FEARLESS

FEAR

LESS

ELVIRA WOODRUFF

SCHOLASTIC INC.

New York   Toronto   London   Auckland
Sydney   Mexico City   New Delhi   Hong Kong

This book was originally published in hardcover by Scholastic Press in 2008.

ISBN 978-0-439-67704-2

Map of England on page 218 by Jim McMahon © Scholastic Inc.

12 11 10

17/0

Printed in the U.S.A.   40
This edition first printing, August 2011

The display type was set in Chorus Girl
The text was set in ITC Cheltenham
Interior book design by Phil Falco
With special thanks to Jackie Worthington from Saffron Walden Museum
for meticulously fact-checking the manuscript, and to Els Rijper from the
Scholastic Photo Research Department for her tenacious search for maps and prints.

This tale owes its telling to:

Alison Barnes, for so generously sharing her expertise on Henry Winstanley's life and times. Her many handwritten letters from across the ocean were invaluable in helping to bring Henry to life. Her encouragement from afar was a gift I will always remember.

Nigel Overton, Maritime Heritage Officer at the Plymouth Museum, Plymouth, England, for patiently answering all of the nautical questions and for his rousing and enlightening lecture about the Eddystone Light on a dark November day in Plymouth.

The helpful and enthusiastic staff at the Saffron Walden Museum for giving me a glimpse of Henry's original drawings and self-portrait.

My fearless and tireless editor, Dianne Hess, who never gives less than her all.

And last but not least, thanks to my research partner, my husband, Joe Pilyar, who boldly took the wheel as we crisscrossed the English countryside in search of a wily ghost.

The very best part of writing this book was the journey we made together to uncover the man behind the light.

For a Dear Fearless Fellow
BENJAMIN JOSEPH WOODRUFF
In His First Year

CONTENTS

PROLOGUE: THE NIGHTMARE
AUTUMN 1703

Eleven-year-old Digory Beale heard his father's death coming under a starless sky. It was not in the roar of the gale on that stormy night, nor in the echo of the sea as it crashed over the ship's starboard bow. It was not in the thunder of the flapping canvas overhead, or in the stunned cry of the ship's first mate as he was blown off deck and swallowed whole in the churning black waters.

Digory Beale heard his father's death coming in the loud creaking and cracking of the ship's floorboards as they were ripped beneath his father's very feet. At the sound of it, Digory's breath caught in his throat. The blood drained from his face, and his heart tightened in his chest, for he was a Cornishman's son and bred to the sea. He knew that the loud crack of wood as it splintered on the jagged jaws of the Eddystone's rocks, fourteen miles from landfall, was every English sailor's nightmare. It was a nightmare from which Digory knew his father would never awaken.

It was startling how fast the water rose up the man's pant legs. The scud and salty spray were already covering him like a shroud when his eyes locked onto the ship's figurehead, a carved wooden angel painted gold, with a broken wing and a trumpet to her lips.

"Have mercy on my soul! See us to safety!" Digory's father pleaded as if the angel could hear him, as if her wings were not made of wood. But she stared vacantly into the waves as if he had no voice, as if he were already dead.

It was then that the man cried out for his eldest son. "Help me, Digory! Help me, please!" But the water was already lapping at Nicholas Beale's mouth. The sting of salt was on his tongue. His final words were muffled as his head slipped under a wave.

"Fight, Father! Fight!" Digory shouted. "Don't let the sea take you!"

Digory's loud outburst was answered with a sharp jab to his side. With one swift kick, his older cousin, Jacca, sent him flying out of the bed. Digory's bare bottom hit the loft's rough floorboards with a thud.

"What's all the noise about?" Jacca mumbled. "Another nightmare?"

Digory blinked and rubbed his eyes. "Aye," he whispered, relieved to be out of his nightmare world and safe and dry in the loft of Aunt Alice's cottage. And quickly he wiggled his way back into the sea of arms and legs in the rickety big bed he shared with his three older cousins.

CHAPTER I: All Hands on Deck

arly the next morning, a heavy fog rolled in off the ocean, swallowing up Mounts Bay and the small granite house that hugged its harbor. Digory awoke to the familiar smells of boys' sweat, fish oil, and turf burning in the fire.

He opened his sea-green eyes and ran his hand through his thick blue-black hair, the color of a mussel shell. The memory of his frightening nightmare had returned.

If he could only stop dreaming about drowning. How could a fisherman's son be so afraid of the sea? He'd always been uneasy when he heard talk of men drowning, but it wasn't until last year that the nightmares began. They started just after his father left Mousehole to take a job on a tall ship.

With their mother long dead, Digory and his nine-year-old brother, Cubby, were sent to live with their aunt Alice and her eleven children. Digory's fears were only made worse by his cousin, Ross, who took great pleasure in scaring Digory with the frightening story of how their grandfather had drowned years before, when his ship wrecked on the Eddystone Reef.

"It was a Plymouth ship," Ross would begin, "newly built with a fine figurehead, a beautiful golden angel. When the ship hit the rocks, the hull split in half. Granddad and all the crew were swept clear out to sea. The only one to make it into shore that night was the broken gold angel floating on the waves." Ross would always pause here and shrug. "What the sea wants, the sea will have. That's what the old salts down at the harbor say."

Now Digory couldn't stop worrying that the sea might want his father. And recently, the closest he would get to the water was to wet his feet as he stood on the beach, drawing with a stick in the sand.

Each season when the mackerel swam into the bay, there was always a call for the boys of Mousehole to man the three-oared jolly boats to bring the fish ashore. Every boy in the village hoped to be picked for the job, but not Digory. Since his father had left, he wanted nothing to do with boats.

Digory yawned and stretched his legs across the bed. His three older cousins were already awake and had long gone down the loft's ladder. Finally he could enjoy the rare pleasure of having the bed all to himself.

But the babies had begun to yowl from below, and soon Aunt Alice would be rapping on the ladder with her iron poker, her signal to get up and do the morning chores. In a family of fourteen, everyone had chores.

Digory reached up to the rafter over the bed and felt in the dark for the old, broken roof slate and piece of cliff chalk he kept there. If he were at home in the rooms his father rented on Quay Street, he could be drawing now. But it was too dark in here. The loft's only window was boarded over with planks. Aunt Alice had covered the glass so as not to have to pay the window tax.

If I were rich as a lord, Digory thought, I'd have windows in every room of my house and big slate walls so I could draw gigantic pictures! He smiled at the luxury of having so much light. But even now in the dark, when he couldn't draw his pictures, he could still imagine them. He pictured himself fighting a fire-breathing dragon, his own green eyes burning with fury as he lifted his sword. In his pictures he was always fearless, fighting beasts and one-eyed giants. In his pictures he was never afraid.

Digory wondered if the sword would be enough to fight the beast. Perhaps he should use a catapult instead. He smiled as he pictured rocks flying through the air toward the fire-breathing dragon. He loved nothing better than to be alone drawing pictures and dreaming up fantastic adventures. But when a boy shares a house with one brother, one aunt, and eleven cousins, he is rarely alone.

"Thundering gales! Look there!" came a voice from under the bed.

"What do you see?" two other voices chimed in.

"Pirates off the starboard!"

"I hate them dirty pirates!"

"I hate them, too! Let's blow them out of the water with a nine gun! *Ka-boom!*"

"Quiet!" Digory hollered down to his brother, Cubby, and his younger cousins, Colan and Gordy, who slept on a straw mat under the bed. They were playing their favorite make-believe game, pretending to be the crew of his father's ship.

"Stop killing pirates and go back to sleep," Digory ordered.

"Hey, you can't kill those pirates with a nine gun," Colan said.

"Yes you can," Gordy answered.

"Could not!"

"Could too!"

"I said quiet!" Digory shouted.

A sudden silence followed, interrupted only by the *scritch-scratch, scritch-scratch* of a mouse scurrying over the floorboards. The cottage was overrun with mice lately. Tam, the old tabby cat, spent all her time sleeping in front of the fire. The mice had grown so bold, they ran circles around her. Aunt Alice wanted to get rid of Tam and complained that she was "useless" and "just another mouth to feed." Digory couldn't help but notice how his aunt's cold gray eyes fell on him when she said this. He knew what she was thinking. He was old enough to be out with the other boys, working on the fishing boats and making a wage. He was as useless as old Tam. If only he wasn't so afraid of the water.

He heard the *scritch-scratch, scritch-scratch* of the mouse again, and he thought about shooting it with his slingshot. It was the best slingshot he had ever made, with a perfect fork and a good piece of leather he'd found on the beach. He decided to wait until light and go on a mouse hunt. Surely Aunt Alice would think that was useful. Just then he felt something graze his leg.

"Agh!" he yelled. But as he looked down, Digory was relieved to see that it was no mouse at all but only a sand crab that scurried over his knee and onto the quilt.

"Cubby! Your crab is loose again," he hollered.

"Oh, Barnacle, you bad crab. I told you to stay put," Cubby scolded as he crawled out from under the bed to retrieve his pet. Digory often wondered how one little red-haired, freckle-faced brother managed to be more troublesome than all eleven of his cousins put together.

"If he gets loose one more time he's going into the pot," Digory threatened.

"Can we come up on deck now?" another little voice begged from below, followed by a fit of coughing. "It's smoky down here."

The chimney in the kitchen was poorly made, and the cottage was always filling with smoke.

"It's just as smoky up here," Digory said. "You stay where you are," he ordered. "I'm the captain of this bed and what I say goes."

The tousled dark hair and sleepy faces of seven-year-old Colan and six-year-old Gordy suddenly appeared beside Cubby. With a sudden loud cry of "All hands on deck!" Cubby led the mutinous crew up and over the sides of the bed, where they gleefully piled on top of their captain.

isobey orders, will ye?" Digory cried out as he fought off the attack with tickles. "Fancy walking the plank, do ye?"

Squeals of laughter and cries begging for mercy were so loud that Digory didn't hear the girls on the loft's ladder.

"We've come with your clothes," ten-year-old Zimmie called over the uproar.

Digory turned to see his cousin's long black braids and ruddy cheeks in the glow of the lamp she set down on a box that served as a table. The smell of fish oil from the lamp's burning wick swirled through the loft. Like most fishermen's families, the Beales depended on the net for their supper, their wages, and even their light.

Zimmie's identical twin, Armynel, followed close behind with a willow basket filled with smoky-smelling shirts and trousers that had dried hard and stiff before the fire. Nightclothes were a luxury a poor man's family could not afford, and underclothes were unheard of. The few times a year their clothes were washed and hung by the hearth to dry, the children went to bed wearing only goose bumps from the cold. Digory pulled the quilt over himself while the others dove under the blanket to hide.

"Smells worse than the backside of Neddy Crumb's pig up here," Zimmie said, making a face.

As she passed by, Cubby reached for Barnacle and quickly attached the crab to one of his cousin's long braids.

"Get it off me!" Zimmie screamed when she looked back to find the crab on her hair. "Get it off!"

Armynel grabbed Barnacle and threw him back onto the bed.

"You needn't be so rough with him," Cubby complained.

"I'm telling Mamm that you've got crabs in the house again, Cubby," Zimmie huffed, smoothing down her hair. "And if you touch my braids once more, I'll drop your breeches into the fire. On my honor, I will!"

"I never touched them, Barnacle did," Cubby grinned.

"'Tis a cold morn to go about the village in naught but your shirt," Armynel said as she dangled a pair of raggedy trousers over the bed.

Digory yanked the trousers from her hand. As the girls hurried back down the ladder, he reached into the basket and began throwing out clothes to his rowdy crew.

"Tar me, Aunt's still not mended the hole," Cubby moaned. He poked his finger through a large hole in the knee of his pants.

"If you can mend a net, you can mend your breeches," Digory told him. He stepped into his own trousers, which he had patched himself with sailcloth. "Besides, Aunt is in a bad enough temper already without you giving her more work."

"If only Father would come home," Cubby sighed.

"I wish *my* father was coming home," Gordy said.

A sudden quiet fell over them. Digory knew that his cousins were thinking of their own father, who had drowned two summers ago when his boat wrecked on the rocks at Lamorna Cove. Aunt Alice had not smiled since.

"You've got your shirt on backwards again, Gordy," Digory said, breaking the silence. He gave his little cousin a playful shove, and soon they were all shoving and shouting again as they tumbled back into a pile on the bed.

"Ross said that when the *Flying Cloud* returns, your father's pockets will be filled with coins," Colan declared as he sat on Gordy's stomach. "You won't be sorry he made the voyage then."

"Uncle Nicholas promised to buy us a goose," Gordy said, pushing Colan off him.

"He promised to bring me a whistle from the other side of the world," Cubby bragged.

"I'd fancy having me a taffy, instead," Gordy said.

"Do you think there are giants on the other side of the world?" Cubby asked. "Like the giant, Mog, in Father's story?"

Digory smiled at the thought of the good tales their father used to tell them. He knew that Cubby's favorite story was the one about Jack the giant killer from Land's End and the giant called Mog, who used the Cornish hills for his table and the stars for his candles.

There was something special in the timber of their father's voice, something steady and strong. But it was his father's singing that Digory missed most. No one could sing a tune like Nicholas Beale. Everyone in the village said so.

At the sudden sound of a noise, Digory turned to see Zimmie back at the ladder.

"What now?" he called to her.

"There is news."

"What news?"

"Mamm's not said yet, but she sent me to fetch you," Zimmie said before disappearing back down the ladder.

"It could be news of the *Flying Cloud*," Colan whispered excitedly.

They had been waiting for months for some word of the ship and her crew. Everyone grew quiet until Cubby let out a loud whoop. "Thundering gales! Father is coming home!" he cried. The others joined in with a chorus of cheers and whistles.

"Don't be gutting your fish before she's in your net," Digory told them. "We've not heard what the news is yet."

But as he walked toward the ladder, Digory hoped they were right. Hadn't his father promised to take him and Cubby back to Quay Street, where they could sit with him by the fire once again and listen to the story of Jack and the giant?

Everyone scrambled toward the ladder. Digory was the first to go down. As his foot reached the bottom rung, he saw his older cousins standing at the hearth. But one look at his aunt's red-rimmed eyes, and his heart stopped. No one needed to tell him that the news was not good.

"Where?" he heard his cousin Jacca ask. "Where did Uncle Nicholas's ship go down?"

CHAPTER III: Stay Away from the Cursed Sea

hey said it went down at Yarmouth," Aunt Alice said, blinking at the shock of hearing her own words. "They said that the *Flying Cloud* went down four and twenty days past, now."

Digory felt the air catch in his throat. He looked around the dimly lit room in disbelief. He could hear the girls' gasps as they reached for each other beside him. He saw Cubby, Colan, and Gordy clumped together in a wide-eyed frozen heap at the bottom of the ladder. Meanwhile Jacca and Ross stared in silence at the dirt floor. Only twelve-year-old Peder, simpleminded from birth, looked unfazed as he sat banging a wooden spoon on his knee.

Baby Bronwyn babbled in the corner. Three-year-old Jane stumbled over her dress and fell down crying. No one moved to pick her up. No one spoke. Digory's worst nightmare was coming true. He couldn't stop his mind from flashing back to the cracking ship filling with water. But this was no dream.

His aunt's worn face crumpled before him as her reddened hands reached numbly to pick up the crying child from the floor.

"Who brought this news?" Jacca asked.

"Jem Sprite," his mother replied weakly. "He heard it from a packhorse driver who journeyed from Plymouth. . . ." Her voice trailed off.

"And the crew, Mamm?" Jacca pressed. "Any saved?"

"He heard no more," his mother said as she broke down in sobs. "Without your uncle's wages we are lost."

Digory closed his eyes. In the stunned silence that followed, his aunt's choked cry rang in his ears.

"My father is coming home," Cubby said in a small voice. "He promised to bring me a whistle."

Aunt Alice sighed loudly. "Promises are like piecrust and easily broken."

Her words fell like a weight on Digory's heaving chest.

"The *Flying Cloud* was a Plymouth ship," he heard Jacca say. "A list of her survivors should be there. One of us must go to Plymouth to learn who survived."

"But there are no boats in the harbor bound for the east," Ross pointed out. "And to go on foot would take weeks. How can we leave our nets now when the fish are coming in?"

No one spoke. Little Jane began to wail.

"Digory will go," Aunt Alice finally said.

"But alone?" Zimmie asked.

Digory's heart pounded in his ears. Plymouth was over

a hundred miles away! He'd never gone more than a few fields from the village.

"'Tis a long journey," Jacca pointed out.

"Digory is old enough," Aunt Alice said. "He should have taken a job on Jory's boat by now. He must go to Plymouth, for we cannot spare another."

"Mamm is right," Ross said. "With the fish coming in, Digory is the only one we can spare."

"Let me go with him," Cubby pleaded.

"Nay, Cubby," Jacca said. "You are too young and would only slow him down. 'Twill be hard enough finding food on the road for one, much less two."

"They say there are highwaymen who prey on travelers," Zimmie whispered.

"His throat could be slit while he slept," Armynel said, her eyes growing wide in the firelight.

Digory swallowed back the lump that was forming in his throat.

"He will not be harmed as long as he is careful," Jacca said, glowering at the twins. He turned to Digory. "You are not afraid, are you, cousin?"

Digory straightened his shoulders.

"Find food where you can in the fields or on the beach," Jacca told him. "But once you are in a town, no matter how hungry you get, you must never steal."

"'Twon't be like it is here in the village," Aunt Alice said darkly. "They show no mercy to thieves in the cities."

"Aye, Aunt." Digory nodded.

"Tim Barley heard tell of a nine-year-old girl in Plymouth who was hung for the crime of pinching her mistress's lace collar," Ross added.

"It would take too long to walk, so you must go by sea," Jacca told him.

When Jacca said "sea," everyone's eyes turned to Digory, for they knew how he feared the water.

"Aye," Digory forced himself to answer.

"Good," Jacca said. "Stay on the coast road. And try to find work on a ship bound for Plymouth. Don't worry. You will find your way."

But as he lay awake in bed that night, Digory worried. He could walk well enough along the road alone. But how was he to overcome his fears and board a ship? All of the men in his family had gone down in boats. How was he ever to trust the sea?

"Digory, are you awake?" Cubby whispered from under the bed. "Let me go with you tomorrow."

"You heard what Jacca said," Digory whispered back. "'Twill be dangerous on the road and you are too young."

"But I am already nine," Cubby protested. "And what if . . . what if . . ."

Digory knew what his brother was thinking. Cubby was only a baby when their mother climbed the bluff to Habbord's cottage to deliver some eggs one summer day, only to fall to her death in the sea. Uncle Kit had left to fish in a nearby cove, only to drown and never return. Now it seemed their father might be gone forever as well. People went away and they never came back. What if Digory were to leave now and never come back?

"I don't want you to go," Cubby pleaded.

Digory scrunched over as far as he could and let Cubby onto the bed. The two curled up together like two snails in a shell and fell into a dreamless sleep.

The next morning, with his slingshot in his back pocket and his slate in one hand, Digory climbed down the loft's ladder. He watched as Aunt Alice packed a small burlap sack with an onion, a crust of barley bread, a salted pilchard, and an old leather flask filled with weak home-made ale. When Digory tried to add his slate, his aunt stopped him.

"There will be no time for your foolish drawings now," she said, taking the old slate and setting it on the table. "Get your head out of the clouds, boy. You'll need all your wits about you for your journey."

Digory nodded dutifully, though his heart sank at the thought of leaving his slate behind.

"I have no coppers to put in your hand," Aunt Alice continued, her voice as somber as the creak of a coffin.

Digory looked down and saw her thin fingers reaching into her apron pocket. "I've only this to give you," she whispered, holding up a tiny, bleached bone. Digory knew at once that it was the bone of a bat, for his aunt often purchased them from the village white witch to use as good-luck charms. He was surprised by this sudden kindness.

"Take it and keep it close for protection. Stay clear of grog houses where brawls brew," she cautioned. "And may the good Saint Julian watch over you."

A chill passed over Digory's heart. For hadn't he heard her say those exact same words to his father before he left? And how had Saint Julian, patron saint of travelers, protected him and the crew of the *Flying Cloud*?

"I have my slingshot," he said, trying to sound brave.

Jacca held out an old horn-handled knife. "You may need this as well."

As Digory put the knife in his sack, the warmth of his cousin's kindness lit up his face until he heard his aunt whisper darkly, "If you do not find your father alive, keep going."

"Keep going?" he repeated. "But where to, Aunt?"

"Anywhere but here," she said. Her voice was so flat and beaten down, he knew enough not to protest. "I can no longer afford to keep you, Digory. There are too many mouths to feed. Come Michaelmas we'll not have a crumb left to eat."

"But what of our pig?" Digory asked.

Aunt Alice shook her head. "The pig is mortgaged. When he is slaughtered the landlord and the miller will take all but the squeak. Without your father's wages I don't know how we shall keep from starving this winter."

Digory lowered his eyes to the dirt floor.

"Now that you are old enough," she continued, "you must seek your fortune in the mines or the fields, anywhere you can, away from the sight of the sea."

"Away from Mousehole?" Digory gasped.

"Aye." She nodded. "Turn away from this cursed sea. For what has it brought us? Nothing but misery and pain, that's what. Why, I've not been able to keep one of my babies' cauls for the five guineas it could bring. We cannot even afford the good luck born us."

Digory knew that the thin membranes covering some of the babies' heads at birth were called cauls. He also knew that people in harbor towns were eager to buy these dried cauls to use as charms to bring good luck, especially in preventing drowning. If only his father had had one with him on the *Flying Cloud*.

"I have no choice," Aunt Alice said, clutching his arm. "The burden of your keep is on you now, nephew." The blood drained from Digory's face. He could feel her long fingernails digging through his thin shirt. "Do not disgrace your family's name."

Digory left the little cottage with Cubby and the younger boys trailing after him. They followed him through the narrow cobbled streets of the village, past the old men sitting beside their fish cellars, past young girls twilling cotton in their doorways, and through the familiar maze of brown nets that were strung from fence posts to dry.

At the village wall they said their last good-byes. As a gaggle of geese noisily pecked the ground, Cubby reached into his shirt and pulled out Digory's broken slate. "I took it when Aunt wasn't looking," he said with an impish smile.

Digory dropped the slate into his sack and hugged his brother to him. How was he to say good-bye? They had never been apart. "Don't worry. I'll come back," he said, fighting the tears that were in his eyes. "And you try and stay out of trouble until I do."

It was there amid the hissing of geese at his ankles and the cries of the gulls overhead that he struck off on his own. He took the pebble-lined path that would lead him out of the West Country and away from the life he had always known.

"Let him be alive," Digory prayed aloud as he felt the rutted clay road beneath his bare feet. "Please the Lord, let my father be alive."

CHAPTER IV: The Crossroads' Corpse

The gulls wheeling overhead were the only company Digory had as he walked the empty road. He looked up at the bright September sun in the wash of blue sky and took a deep breath of the salty air.

He tried not to think of his nightmare or how fearful he felt as he walked alone. He would have to pretend to be brave until he got to Plymouth.

I know I will find Father, he reassured himself. *And we will return home together.* He would focus on the light and push away all dark thoughts. It was the only way he could go on.

The road itself was not much wider than a footpath, and soon Digory was walking at a good clip. He hurried past the Cornish hedges of stone that outlined hills covered with gorse so golden it hurt his eyes.

He heard rooks in the elm trees and the song of wrens in the blackthorns. He walked over cliffs that looked down on black-pebbled beaches edged with ribbons of white foam. He passed by a field of heather that was such a startling haze of pink it made his heart sing.

He stood aside to let an old gypsy shuffle by, leading a pack of goonhillies laden with sacks of tea. Their saddles were decorated with brightly colored ribbons and bells that made a pleasing tinkle as the ponies tripped lightly over the stony road.

By midday Digory was hungry, and he stopped by a low, moss-covered wall. He sat down and removed a small pebble that had stuck in between his swollen toes. It felt good to rest. He took a drink from his flask and cut a piece of the fish from the sack. The air was still until a low whining sound broke through the quiet, followed by a sharp rustling in the bushes.

Digory froze. Was it a highwayman? Was it a smuggler? As the noise grew louder, he imagined a bloodthirsty scoundrel preparing to attack him. He reached into his sack and gripped the knife's handle. He held his breath and watched as the bushes stirred, and suddenly a sad, shaggy brown face appeared looking back at him. It was Fishbone, the village stray, who slept under boats, took his meals from the gutter, and drank from mud puddles. Digory had always thought Fishbone the most noble and friendly of dogs, and he couldn't have been happier to see him.

"Fishbone!" Digory cried. "What are you doing here?" He jumped off the wall and hugged the scruffy dog to him. Then he pulled the bread from his sack and broke off a bit of the crust. Fishbone gobbled it up and licked his hand clean.

"That's all I can spare for now," Digory said. He picked up a stick and threw it.

Fishbone ran for the stick and brought it back, dropping it at Digory's feet. He panted happily as he sank down beside Digory to rest.

"You've come a long way," Digory said, stroking his matted fur. "But Plymouth is farther still. Are you sure you want to come along on such a long journey? It'll not be easy, and there's no guarantee of what vittles we'll find along the way."

Fishbone put his head on Digory's knee.

"You're on your own, just as I am," Digory said, scratching the dog's neck. "But together it won't be so lonely, will it?"

Fishbone cocked his head, whined twice, then barked.

"Then it's settled," Digory said. "You're coming with me!" And together the two started happily down the road. Fishbone stopped every now and again to sniff a mole's burrow or lick a clump of manure. But as they rounded a sharp bend at a crossroads, the dog began to snort and growl. Then he sat down and refused to go on.

"What is it, boy?" Digory whispered.

Fishbone looked toward the trees and answered with a loud, steady bark. Digory looked around uneasily.

"Come on, Fishbone, there's nothing there. Let's go." Digory took a few steps forward, but the dog wouldn't budge and continued to bark.

"Oh, all right, be stubborn, if you must. But I haven't all day to wait here," Digory finally said, nudging Fishbone out of his way and walking ahead. But as he came to the bend in the road, Digory heard the loud creak of a chain and the flapping of wings overhead.

Looking up, he stopped dead in his tracks, too horrified to move. For there, swaying in the breeze beside the road, was the reason for Fishbone's warnings. It was a rotting corpse swinging from a wooden crossbar, with two large crows pecking away at the eyeless head!

CHAPTER V: A Meeting with Master Death

igory cried out and squeezed his eyes shut tight. He remembered the stories he'd heard of thieves and smugglers who found themselves left swinging from the gibbet chains at crossroads throughout the countryside.

Digory opened his eyes slowly and took another look at the lifeless body that had once been a living man. He knelt down beside Fishbone, who was panting at his side.

"Seems our friend here has run out of time," a voice cooed from behind him. Digory spun around to see a pasty-faced man dressed in a long, dirty, tattered green coat. The fellow had a large wooden box strapped to his back and on his head he wore the tallest black hat Digory had ever seen. He was a stick of a man with crowlike features, a sharp, beaky nose, and scraggly black whiskers on his pointy chin. But the most startling thing of all about the stranger was the loud *tick, tick, tick* that came from under his coat.

"Allow me to introduce myself," he said as he tipped his hat. "Master Jonathan Death, at your service."

Fishbone sniffed the man's boots, then took off into the brush.

"Poor devil, hey?" Master Death said, with a nod to the corpse. "He was probably strung up for some small infraction, stealing a loaf or poaching a hare. These are unforgiving times we live in, lad. I've come across many a crossroad corpse in my line of work."

The chains creaked above them as the corpse swung eerily in a sudden gust of wind. Digory winced as he saw the smile of a skeleton imprinted in the rotting flesh. He quickly looked back to the stranger. "Your line of work, sir?"

"Time, my boy, time." Jonathan Death smiled and opened his coat to reveal a crimson lining completely covered in pocket watches, all of which were ticking loudly. "I travel the land selling timepieces. And your name, lad?"

"Beale, sir," Digory answered, unable to take his eyes off the shiny, egg-shaped watches. "Digory Beale."

"Yes, I deal in time, as you can see," the man continued. "And I ask you, Digory Beale, what more satisfying transaction might a man make than to buy a bit of time from Master Death himself? How many would give their eyeteeth to strike such a bargain? I'll warrant our friend here would have been more than eager to do such business." He tipped his hat to the corpse. "But alas, his time has all run out."

Digory looked back up at the corpse and gulped.

"So on to new ventures and living customers, I say," Jonathan Death continued cheerily, placing his hat back on his head. "Are you from these parts, Digory Beale?"

"I come from the village of Mousehole, sir. I am on my way east to look for my father in Plymouth Town."

Jonathan Death's dark eyebrows lifted. "I see. And would you be in the market for a little time yourself, Master Beale?" asked the salesman optimistically. "Might you have a small savings put away for just such an opportunity?"

"No, none, sir," Digory told him.

"I was afraid of that." Master Death frowned as he buttoned up his worn coat. "This wild countryside is hardly conducive to commerce. Have you nothing, lad? No item of worth you might trade for a timepiece?"

Digory never dreamed of owning something as precious as a clock. But the idea took hold of him now, and he suddenly wanted one more than anything. He reached into his sack and pulled out the tiny bat bone his aunt had given him.

"'Tis meant to bring good fortune," Digory said hopefully.

But Master Death looked at the tiny bone and shook his head. "I believe a man makes his own good fortune. You'll have to do better than that."

Disappointed, Digory dug into the sack again, and before he could stop himself, he pulled out Jacca's knife.

"Will this do, sir?"

There was a flicker of light in Master Death's gray eyes as he spotted the knife's finely crafted horn handle. "Now that is more like it," he said in a honeyed voice. "Of course, it is of poor quality," he hurried to add. "And you'd be hard put to get more than a few pence for it on a London street. But lucky for you, we're not in London and I'm in the mood for a bit of bargaining."

He quickly snatched Digory's knife from his hand and it disappeared into one of his many pockets. "Here you are," he said, reaching back into his coat and producing a small brass watch gear. "Your very own piece of time," he declared, handing it to Digory.

"But this is no timepiece," Digory objected.

"*Au contraire,* my young friend," Master Death replied smoothly. "'Tis a piece of time to be sure, for no watch can run without its gears."

Digory's fingers trembled as he held the gear out before him. "I wish for my knife back, sir. My cousin gave it to me for my journey. I never meant to trade it for something as useless as this."

The watch salesman shrugged. "'Twas as fair a transaction as any in Piccadilly," he said, giving Digory a sideways look. He scratched the stubble on his pointy chin as the boy bit his lip. "But then we are a goodly distance from city ways." With that he pulled the knife out of his pocket and handed it back to Digory. "You've much to learn about the ways of the world, my young friend. A man should never be so quick to part with those things he holds most dear."

Digory handed back the gear and slid the knife safely into the bottom of his sack as Master Death looked on with a smile. Although he was certainly strange and crafty, Digory thought he saw kindness in the man's face.

"Well, we've been dawdling here as if we had all the time in the world," Master Death declared. "Since I am bound for the west and you for the east, this is where we must part. I bid you a safe journey."

"And you as well, sir," Digory answered. He turned to look for Fishbone, who had wandered off into the woods, but before either could take a step, two men sprang out at them from the bushes.

Digory felt his heart stop at the sight of them. One had a deeply pocked face and a dagger in his hand. The other came at them with a toothless grin and a long-nosed pistol.

"Prepare for a voyage, ma dears, 'tis the King's Navy come calling," the man with the gun croaked in a voice as creaky as the rusted gibbet chain over their heads.

CHAPTER VI: A Last Look at the World

Jonathan Death's face turned as ashen as the barrel of the pistol that was pressed to his head. Digory's knees nearly buckled beneath him. Like everyone in Cornwall, Digory had heard of the press-gangs who were paid to kidnap boys and men and force them into the navy. If only he could get to Jacca's knife or his slingshot!

"Didn't I say today would be our lucky day, Cribbs?" the man with the pistol crowed.

"Aye, Will, that ye did." The other snorted as he placed the cold blade of his dagger against Digory's throat. "For it looks as if we've snagged two recruits for the good ship *Half Moon*. Be a good lad now and hand over that sack."

Digory froze.

"Be quick about it," the man snapped.

With a shaky hand Digory held out his sack. The man pulled out the flask and took a drink but quickly spit it out. "Never could abide six-water grog," he said, screwing up his face. "Not enough spirit in it to swear by."

"What else has he got in there?" the other man demanded.

"Just a piece of broken slate," his partner muttered. "And this," he said, holding up the knife. His face broke into a grin. "With it we can buy us a proper jug of mahogany to drink our good fortune."

Digory cringed at the stale stink of mahogany, the drink made from gin and treacle that was already on his captors' breath.

"Aye, 'tis a lucky day, indeed," the man with the pistol declared. "But give a listen. Wot's all that tickin' about?" His grizzled cheek twitched as he leaned in closer to Jonathan Death.

" 'Tis the tick of time," the salesman answered. "And if you would but allow me to open my coat . . ."

"Open yer coat, hey?" The thug narrowed his eyes. "I would fancy takin' a squint inside, but no surprises, for me trigger finger 'as a powerful itch, it does."

"Be no trouble to slice off the boy's nose, if'in they did pull any tricks," Cribbs said matter-of-factly. Digory winced as Cribbs brought the blade of the knife up, just under his nose. It smelled of iron and blood.

"No need for that. There'll be no tricks," Master Death assured them. He slowly opened his coat. "I only wish to show you my wares."

"Lor's alive!" Cribbs cried. "Why, I never seed so many timepieces in all me livin' days!"

"It would be my pleasure to give you one in exchange for my freedom and the boy's as well," Master Death offered.

Digory gave him a grateful glance. Maybe there was a way out after all.

"You'll not find a better timepiece in all of London, I promise you," Master Death continued smoothly.

"I always did fancy having me such a timepiece," the man with the pistol said.

But Cribbs looked confused. "Wot of the seven pounds we was goin' to collect for bringing the two of them in? And the jug we was goin' to buy?"

"Seven pounds!" his partner shot back. "What's that compared to the worth of all of these?" He reached out to finger the watches greedily.

Jonathan Death's eyes nervously followed the man's grubby fingers. "I offered *one*," he reminded him.

"And not a very generous offer now, was it, ma dear?" his captor snarled. "Nay, I think we'll 'ave 'em all. That way there's one for me and one for my dear friend, Master Cribbs here, and all the rest left over to sell and make a tidy sum."

"But . . . but that's robbery!" Master Death stammered.

"He's right, Will," Cribbs said, spitting onto the ground. "Collectin' bounty, that's legal, edn't? But if we was to rob 'em and leave 'em, and they was to tell anyone, why 'twould get us the gibbet chains, that's sure."

"You've straw in yer head for brains, man!" his partner snapped. "'Aven't I always had a gift for solutions? And 'aven't I come up with the perfect solution for us now?"

"'Av'ee, Will?" Cribbs asked hopefully.

"Aye, and 'tis simple, really." He lowered his voice to a gargley whisper. "All we 'ave to do is to fix it so they never talk again."

"But how are we to do that, Will?"

"Why, we kill 'em, of course!"

Cribbs's face brightened on hearing this. "Oh, aye, ye do have a gift for solutions!"

Digory felt his knees turn to jelly.

"I pray you," Jonathan Death pleaded, his voice not nearly as smooth as before, "do not give in to this treachery you plan. For surely it is the devil's work."

"Hold ye' greasy tongue, watchman, or I'll 'ave it cut out and fried for me breakfast," his captor barked, poking Jonathan Death's head with the nose of his gun. "And as for the devil, why, every man knows he'll not show hisself in Cornwall for fear of being put into a pasty." He laughed loudly at the old joke.

"Hang on there, Will," Cribbs said, suddenly frowning. "How will I be able to tell if me new timepiece is working if I cannot read it? I never did learn to do sums."

"You've only to put it up to your ear to hear it ticking. That's how you know it's working, you fool," his partner snapped.

Cribbs smiled again. "Lord love ye, Will. Ye think of everything, ye do."

He turned to Digory and pressed the dagger to his neck. "Shall I slit his throat right 'ere?" he asked eagerly.

Digory took one last look at the world, shut his eyes tight, and prayed for it to be over quickly.

CHAPTER VII: Time to Go

Digory dared not breathe for fear of the dagger that rested on his throat. And he felt himself grow faint when the man with the pistol whispered, "Nay, Cribbs, not 'ere. We'll take 'em into the wood and kill 'em where no one can see."

Digory tripped and fell to his knees as he was pushed forward into a grove of trees. But Cribbs quickly yanked him up again. From behind them, the constant *tick, tick, tick* told Digory that Master Death and his captor were near.

As Cribbs shoved him up against a tree, Digory closed his eyes and began to pray. *Let it be quick, Lord. I pray you, let it be quick!* But nothing happened.

Suddenly there was a rustling noise in the brush, and Digory's eyes flew open. Cribbs let go of his neck and turned to stare into the weeds. Digory hesitated for a second. He knew it might be his only chance to get away. He also knew it might get him killed. There was no time to think it over. He slid down and away from the tree and ran off as fast as he could.

"Where the devil do you think you're going?" Cribbs cried, taking off after him.

"Help!" Digory shouted at the top of his lungs. He ran dazed through the woods until he heard a dog's bark, then headed toward the sound.

"Heigh-ho!" a man called, bursting out of the brush.

"What mischief is this?" shouted another, running toward Cribbs.

"Drop your weapons, you blackhearts!" a third man commanded.

Digory was overjoyed to see Fishbone, accompanied by three burly young farmers with pitchforks and rakes, charging after the thugs. The man with the gun aimed and pulled the trigger, but the gun never went off. He and Cribbs, seeing that they were defenseless and outnumbered, quickly released their prisoner and darted into the woods.

"Have they done ye harm?" a young farmer asked as he offered his arm to Master Death.

"They were going for our throats!" Jonathan Death replied breathlessly. He turned to Digory. "If you hadn't taken the chance and run, we'd be dead now. I owe you my life, lad!"

"My cousins warned me of such men," Digory said, rubbing his shoulder where the man had grabbed him.

"They're a bad lot, them two," one of the farmers said. "My brothers and I have seen the press-gangs skulkin' about the village."

"Press-gang turned to thieves and murderers," Jonathan Death added.

The young man's brow furrowed. "Begging your pardon, sir, but what's that ticking?"

Jonathan Death's gray eyes brightened under his tall black hat. "I thought you'd never ask," he said as he opened his coat.

Meanwhile, Digory sank down beside Fishbone, who was sniffing his feet.

"Oh, am I glad to see you, Fishbone," he murmured into the dog's fur. "You're my good-luck dog, you are."

"Aye, lad," one of the farmers said. "That he is. I was hunting hare when I saw him running toward me. He led me here, and when I saw the mischief that was afoot I called my brothers from their field."

"I'd be happy to offer each of you a timepiece at half the cost by way of my thanks for saving our lives," Master Death suggested. Though he only had one taker, he advised the others to save up and promised to pass by again in twelve months' time.

Then he closed up his coat, and he and Digory headed back to the crossroads. Digory found the flask Aunt Alice had given him, but the sack was gone. Not only had he lost his knife and his slate, but what little food he had was gone as well.

As he looked at the empty road before him, Digory suddenly wished he were traveling west with Jonathan Death rather than east to Plymouth with only an old dog at his side.

"You and your friend there are welcome to join me on my way to Land's End," Master Death offered as if reading his thoughts. Although Digory wished he could say yes, he knew it was the wrong direction.

"Thank you, sir, but we are Plymouth-bound." Then he told him about the *Flying Cloud* and how he hoped to find his father.

Jonathan Death smiled. "A good man always follows his heart." He slipped the box off his back and pulled out a small loaf of bread.

"Here's a little something to tide you over on your journey," he said, handing Digory the loaf. "But have a care, lad. Stay out of the open and sleep undercover when you can, for I'll wager those cowardly rogues will not have gotten very far. We were lucky this time."

"Not lucky enough to keep my cousin's knife," Digory said sadly as he fingered the loaf.

"It's a come-and-go world we live in," the watchman said with a shrug. Then he reached into his coat, took out one of his watches, and handed it to Digory.

"A small memento of our time together." Master Death smiled.

Digory was stunned. "A timepiece for me? To keep?" He had never owned anything of such worth.

"Let it be a reminder to you, my young friend. Never take your days for granted, for you never know when the wheel will stop. You never know when your hours will end. A pleasure spending time with you, Master Digory Beale." He tipped his high black hat and stepped lightly back on the road.

Digory watched him walk off into the fiery pink sunset as the loud *tick, tick, tick* from under his coat grew fainter and fainter.

"Have a look at this, Fishbone," Digory whispered excitedly. He held the watch in front of his companion's shaggy face. "Have you ever seen anything so fine?"

Fishbone sniffed the watch and tried to lick it.

"'Tis not to eat, you silly dog," Digory said, pulling back the timepiece. As he ran his fingers over the smooth glass face, his eyes took in every detail. The shiny brass back, the two black arrows that turned on their own, and the numbers in a fancy black script. He wondered what each stood for. He had never been to school and never studied his letters or his sums. But he was thrilled to have the watch nonetheless.

As he turned it over in his hands, Digory thought of all the barley, milk, and eggs Aunt Alice would be able to barter for with such a fine thing. Yes, with such a bounty, Digory could return home a hero! But first he must find his father.

Carefully, he slipped the watch into his pocket. As Fishbone wandered around in the weeds, Digory looked up to the sky. He needed no timepiece to tell him what time it was. The sun sat low on the horizon, and he knew what little daylight was left them.

"Time to go, Fishbone," he called. "Time to go."

Digory walked hopefully toward Plymouth as his dog trotted contentedly behind him.

CHAPTER VIII: Followed

s happy as he was to be alive and unharmed, Digory was still shaken from his brush with mortal danger. And as darkness began to blanket the hill, it took all of his courage to keep going. His ears pricked up at every sound. His eyes darted at every shadow. And he froze in his tracks when he heard a fox running swiftly through some gorse.

"Come back, boy!" Digory called as Fishbone tore off after the fox. Spooked by the loud hoot of an owl, Digory picked up a big stick on the side of the road to use as a weapon.

After several minutes Fishbone returned and joined Digory once more. And the two continued on their way. The sun was sinking quickly, and the dark sky was smudged with gray clouds. A damp breeze worked its way under his shirt, and his skin tingled with goose bumps. And even though the empty road stretched out before him, Digory couldn't shake the uneasy feeling that those two terrible men were still loose in the woods. What if they came back for him?

The darkening fields shimmered with the blue iridescent light from the glowworms that hung from the hedgerows. A sad-faced moon rose up over the hills. Fishbone stayed close and blinked at the wind that was whipping around them.

It was then that Digory remembered the stories of witches that his neighbor, old Madgy Godwin, often told as she smoked her long clay pipe before her cottage door.

"If it's witches ye want to see," old Madgy would cackle, "ye can spy 'em by the light of the glowy worms they use to guide 'em over the hills."

The thought of witches in that lonely landscape sent shivers down Digory's spine. In fact his thoughts of witches proved too much for him, and when he spotted a haystack in the distance, he dropped the stick he was carrying and broke into a run, hurrying to reach cover.

Fishbone never left his side as Digory sank down beside a stack of hay. Fishbone sniffed all around the edges of the hay and began to growl.

"Quiet," Digory whispered.

Fishbone continued to growl. Then Digory saw five new kittens curled up in the straw next to them.

"Leave them be. Their mother must be out hunting some mice for their supper," he whispered. A sadness tugged at him as he thought how lucky those kittens must be to have a mother to feed them. He missed Cubby and his cousins. And he missed his father most of all.

He pulled Fishbone to the other side of the haystack, then gathered up some straw to make a bed. The dog gave a halfhearted bark before pacing in a circle and curling up beside Digory with a loud sigh. They lay cuddled together in each other's warmth. But suddenly Fishbone pricked up his ears. He jumped to his feet and began to bark and bark and bark.

Digory froze at the sound of twigs snapping on the other side of the haystack. Was it the two thugs who had attacked him before? Would they slit his throat this time? He prayed for Fishbone to stop barking. The dog was going to give him away!

Digory reached for his slingshot. The seconds crept by as the rustling sound of footsteps grew louder and louder. Then Fishbone darted to the other side of the stack. He bounded up to the intruder, lunged at the dark figure, and knocked him over.

"Tar me, Fishbone!" a small voice exclaimed.

"Cubby!" cried Digory. "Cubby, is that you?"

CHAPTER IX: Cousin to a Witch

Digory ran around the haystack. He hooted with joy as he hugged his little brother tight. Fishbone wagged his tail and jumped up on Cubby, licking his face and almost knocking him over.

"Digory! Digory! I'm so glad to see you!" Cubby cried.

Digory couldn't stop the grin that was spreading across his face. He was never so happy to see anyone in all his life. "I'm glad to see you, too, but you know 'twas wrong to leave against Aunt Alice's wishes."

"I'm sorry for it," Cubby said. "But she'll be happy to be rid of me. She said there were too many mouths to feed at home. Besides, she'll be pleased when we bring back Father with his pockets full of silver. Then she can make us the biggest Starry Gazzey pasty you ever did see."

Starry Gazzey pasty was the children's favorite pie, with the pilchard fish baked whole in the center, their big goggly eyes gazing up at the stars.

"There you go again, filling your nets before they're in the water," Digory said, shaking his head. "We've a long way to travel, and you can't stay up all night jabbering away."

"I'll be quiet as a clam from now on," Cubby said, rubbing Fishbone's head. "But have you anything to eat or drink? For I've a powerful hunger and my throat is so dry."

Digory led the way around the haystack and handed his brother the flask. "But not too much," he said, "for we'll need to make it last." Then he broke off a piece of the bread and watched as Cubby gobbled it down. "How close behind did you follow? Did you meet anyone on the road?"

"No," he said. "I had to walk Colan and Gordy back home so they'd not follow me. I only saw some tinners covered in dust and a sheepherder with a bad stink on him. Oh, and a body left to rot at the crossroads. Oh, Digory, he had no eyes! And his face was but a skull!"

Digory nodded. "I saw it, too. It was there at the crossroads I met Master Death and a pair of murderous scoundrels who tried to kill us."

Cubby leaned forward to listen as Digory related the frightening encounter. He finished by letting Cubby hold the watch. But at the memory of his brush with death, Digory grew uneasy again. He wished they could turn around and go back home. If only they didn't have to make the long journey to Plymouth! The two grew quiet as an owl hooted in the distance and the wind whooshed its way through the gorse.

" 'Tis a big world, Cubby, bigger than I ever imagined," Digory said, slipping the watch back into his pocket. "And there are all kinds of men in it, not just fishermen, like back in Mousehole. Once we reach Plymouth, why, there's no telling what we will find."

"I hope we'll find Father," Cubby said as he sank down into the straw.

"Aye," Digory answered softly. The hoot of the owl rippled through the darkness and the kittens mewed fearfully. Digory began to sing their father's favorite shanty, the one he'd sang to comfort them on the coldest, darkest nights, and Cubby joined in.

"Dance to your daddy,
My little laddie.
Dance to your daddy,
My little man.
Thou shall have a fish,
Thou shall have a fin,
Thou shall have a haddock,
When the boat comes in."

As the two brothers sang, the wind continued to blow off the sea. It blew off the waves of Mounts Bay, sweeping east over the moonlit fields of Trewa. It whipped its way around elms and oaks and nosed into the cracks and crannies of every cobb cottage in its path.

"There are dark days ahead," the wind shrieked. *"They head into a storm."*

CHAPTER X: Come Aboard, Me Hearties

Early the next morning, Digory, Cubby, and Fishbone trekked down the narrow rutted path that made up the road in these parts. Along the way Cubby almost got stung by some angry wasps whose nest he had poked with a stick. He got his foot caught in a rabbit's hole, and he was about to eat a poison mushroom he found growing under a tree when Digory stopped him.

"Will you just stay on the road and keep walking?" Digory said, exasperated. "We'll never get there if you keep getting into trouble. I'm having a hard enough time figuring out the right way to go without having to watch you every minute."

There were no signposts or markers to guide them. The position of the sun and the sight of the sea from the cliff were all Digory had to tell him they were headed in the right direction. The morning air was full of birdsong, and the boys took turns identifying the *tee-seep, tee-seep* of the lark and the *maag, maag, maag* of the magpie.

Fishbone chased a rabbit into a field, disappearing in the high grass, only to reappear minutes later. Together the three walked on until they came to a hillside that shimmered green, golden, and pink in the morning's half-light. The beauty of the land seemed almost magical to Digory, but beauty was no consolation for an empty stomach, and Cubby did not hesitate to complain.

"I'm so hungry I could eat the barnacles off a hull," he moaned. "Why, there's not even a turnip to pull from a field."

"Jacca said to stick to the road and we'd find a cove," Digory reminded him. "We must keep going."

But he worried that Cubby was right. With no farms in sight and nothing but wild hillsides before them, they had little chance of finding food. They pushed on for many more miles of road until they came to the edge of a cliff.

"Look there!" Cubby cried, pointing to the beach below.

Digory looked down to find two large ships anchored just outside the harbor.

"Pray that one is headed east," Cubby said.

Digory frowned as the reality began to sink in. They would have to board a boat to get to Plymouth. There was no other way.

"You mustn't think of your nightmares. . . ." Cubby began, when he saw Digory's troubled face.

"Let's go," Digory said, starting down the cliff.

When they reached the beach, they found that it was covered with drift nets, corks, and lead sinkers.

"Please, sir," Digory called out to a passing fisherman. "Can you tell us if there are any boats in the harbor heading east?"

"Aye, lad." The fisherman shifted his heavy brown nets from one shoulder to the other. "They say the *Elizabeth* of Bristol will be making for Plymouth Dock this day." He pointed to one of the tall ships anchored on the edge of the harbor. "Their jolly boat is just come in and is loading some hogsheads filled with our own fair maidens."

Digory saw three men loading the adjacent jolly boat with wooden barrels filled with the dried and salted pilchard fish, called "fair maidens."

"They even paid a fair price for some rabble fish for the captain's table," the fisherman said.

Digory thanked the man, and he and Cubby ran to the jolly boat. There they found a stocky, bulldog-faced man with black sideburns who seemed to be in charge. He shouted orders to two young sailors as they rolled a keg over a wooden plank onto the boat.

"Quit your widdy-waddying about, you lazy scrubs," the man barked. "We've a hard sail before us, and the captain will be in a black temper if we keep him waiting much longer."

"Begging your pardon, sir," Digory spoke up. "But I was wondering if we could come aboard the *Elizabeth*, as far as Plymouth Dock?"

The man shrugged. "That depends if you've the silver to cross my hand."

"We've no silver, but we can work for our passage," Digory told him.

"I can lift a meal sack weighing six stone," Cubby bragged.

"We can scrub your decks and polish your brass," Digory offered. "Or skin and gut the fish for your captain's supper. We are both hardy and willing to work."

"Hardy, you say?" The man snorted. "Why you're thin as herring bones, the pair of you! One good gale could lift you off deck and blow your skinny carcasses clear 'round the Barbary Coast!"

The other sailors laughed at this remark, and Digory was about to give up when he heard the man say, "But 'twould put me in the cook's good favor to give him some extra hands. And if this boat is not loaded soon, we'll not make the tide." He turned to the boys and shook his head. "All right then, me hearties, you can come aboard, after you help loading them kegs."

*　　*　　*

An hour later, the three travelers found themselves on the gleaming white foredeck of the mighty *Elizabeth* as she put out for the open sea. The ship was massive, with thirty sails and a mainmast towering nearly two hundred feet abovedecks.

Cubby was beside himself with joy, for unlike Digory he loved the sea and hoped to be a sailor himself one day. But Digory decided that the only way to quiet his fears was to keep his eyes and his mind off the water. He concentrated instead on Fishbone, who, with tail between his legs, had slithered behind a large coil of rope. With every creak and sway of the ship, Digory felt sick to his stomach and feared that the boat would pitch him into the sea. He wished he could crawl beside Fishbone and hide.

Bells rang and orders were shouted as lines were pulled and sailors raced up and down the ratlines to make the most of the morning's strong westerly wind. One by one the huge sails unfurled. The topsails were set first, then the jibs, then the topgallants. The big courses followed. Braces, sheets, and tacks hummed with the strain.

Digory and Cubby stood close as the ship picked up speed and the sea rose up in gleaming blue hills. Neither of them had ever been on such a large vessel, and Cubby's eyes were big and round as the Spanish coin Jacca had once found on the beach. As seasick as Digory felt, he was also sick with worry. He couldn't stop thinking of his nightmares. He felt like retching each time the ship pitched to the left or the right. And he worried about finding his father in Plymouth.

The cook set a large bucket of fish down before the boys and handed them each a biscuit. "So you don't go fainting on me, afore you get me fish gutted," he said, giving them each a knife.

Digory bit into his biscuit. Perhaps if he ate something it would calm his unsettled stomach. When no one was looking he tossed bits of fish and guts to Fishbone, who gulped them down greedily.

"Digory," Cubby called. "Look at how high the crow's nest is!"

Digory followed Cubby's gaze up to the small lookout platform perched far above them on the ship's mast. It was so high up it made him dizzy. He looked back down and an image from his nightmare rose up in his mind. It was the sea sweeping over the deck as the loud crack of the hull echoed in his ears. He blinked, and the terrible image was gone.

"It must be a mile or more up in the sky," Cubby said. "Wouldn't it be heaven to watch the waves from way up there?"

Digory said nothing as he stared down at his biscuit.

"I could climb up there easy!" Cubby declared.

"I'd fancy seeing that," a nearby sailor snickered. He looked to be only a few years older than Digory and was dressed in a striped shirt and dirty white duck trousers. The boy had such an unfriendly smirk on his sunburnt face that Digory took an immediate dislike to him.

"You landlubbers haven't the nerve to climb up to a crow's nest," he added.

"Who says?" Cubby called after him.

"I say," the boy shot back. "For what would you know of climbing a ship's rigging?"

"Back in Mousehole we climb cliffs that are higher than that," Cubby bragged.

"I've a penny in my locker says you ain't got the nerve," the boy taunted.

A couple of sailors, hearing the challenge, drew closer.

"I'll wager I can," Cubby said as a larger group gathered.

"Cubby, what have you done?" Digory whispered as the boy ran belowdecks to get his penny.

"It weren't all a tale," Cubby said with a guilty look. "We do climb some of the cliffs back home."

"But we've never climbed the high ones!" Digory reminded him. "And even if we had, that rigging is no cliff! And you've no penny to wager with. Your blabbering jaw has gotten you into a pretty piece of trouble now."

Cubby rubbed his tongue under his chipped tooth, the way he always did when he was nervous. "What will we do?" he whispered.

"You'll keep your jaw still, that's what you'll do," Digory ordered.

"I've a gold guinea that says the little landlubber falls afore he reaches the jib lines," a burly sailor shouted.

"I say he makes it to the foresail afore he tumbles," another cried. Soon more and more coins were held up, as the crew was eager to brighten the monotony of their work with a contest.

Digory was suddenly woozy as he looked back up into the network of ratlines that seemed to stretch into the clouds. He knew Cubby could never climb the rigging. He was too small and would kill himself trying.

"Come now, landlubber, time to lay your money down," the boy demanded on his return to the deck. "Where's your penny?"

"He has no coin," Digory told him. "He made a mistake."

The boy's eyes narrowed. "Do you know what happens to those who place false bets onboard this ship? The quartermaster gives their backs a striping with a salted rope."

Digory put his arm protectively around Cubby's shoulders. "He's not yet ten years old," he pleaded.

"Old enough to make a wager, old enough to keep it," a sailor said as he mopped the deck.

Digory could feel Cubby trembling under his arm. "I'll take his wager for him," he said.

But the sailor boy shook his head no. "You didn't make the bet. He did."

"I am his brother," Digory insisted. "We are blood, and I've the right to climb in his stead. I'll keep his wager."

"All right, but where's your penny, then?"

Digory hesitated. "I have none," he admitted.

"Just as I thought." The boy smirked.

"But he does have a dog," another sailor said.

"A dog would be good company for us on board," said another.

"All right, the dog it is," the sailor boy said.

Digory looked up to the crow's nest that seemed to rise as high as the clouds. He had to protect Cubby and Fishbone. Then he scanned the deck, looking for the captain or the sailor with the bulldog face. He hoped that one of them might make everyone go back to work and put a stop to the wager. But the captain was belowdecks, and when the bulldog-faced sailor appeared and was told of the contest, he quickly produced two coins from his pocket in order to place a bet of his own!

The sailors' shouts soon filled the air as word spread

among the crew. Men began betting their week's wages on whether the "landlubber" would live or die when he fell.

"Here, take this," Cubby whispered as he pressed a small pebble into Digory's hand. "It's my lucky stone."

Digory gave out a little whimper as he shoved the pebble into his pocket. For as he looked up at the rigging and the huge, billowing white sails, he knew that he'd need more than a stone to help him now. Unlike the cliffs that he was used to climbing back home, there would be no ledges here to break a fall. And there was the wind to contend with, a wind so powerful it could easily blow a boy off the ropes, like a leaf blown off a tree.

What if he couldn't hold on? What if he fell into the water? He was sure a fall from that height would take him to the bottom of the ocean.

"What's the matter, landlubber? Turning coward? If you won't climb, we'll have to take it out on your little brother's hide," the boy jeered.

This last taunt was the final nudge that pushed Digory into action.

"The only thing lost will be your penny," Digory shot back. He took a step, grabbed the rigging, and started to climb.

CHAPTER XI: Up to the Crow's Nest

s the sailors shouted out their bets, Digory gripped the rigging. But his feet weren't used to the feel of the ratlines that went up the mast like a ladder. He missed a rung and almost pitched onto the deck! The crew's laughter rang in his ears as he began to climb, ten feet, twenty feet. He continued to go up, thirty feet, forty feet, higher and higher, till the only thing he could hear was the thunder of the sails in the wind.

Don't look down, Digory said to himself as he stopped, exhausted, to rest. He looked up instead, but his heart sank at the sight of the crow's nest, which still seemed to be perched high above him. He continued to climb, fifty feet, sixty feet, higher and higher as the coarse rope blistered the skin of his hands. Panting for breath, he stopped to watch a seagull fly effortlessly by.

I wish I had your wings, Digory thought. He continued to go up, seventy feet, eighty, ninety, one hundred. "Mustn't look down! Mustn't look down!" His voice was now no more than a squeak carried off in the monstrous boom of the wind. The gale had become so fierce the ship was listing into the waves. Digory had to fight the sway of the ropes that threatened to toss him into the sea.

His hands gripped the rigging so tightly, they began to bleed. A wave of dizziness overtook him. He reeled to the left and then to the right. And then he did the one thing he had promised himself he would not do. He lowered his head and looked down. The sight of the choppy waves below him made him instantly dizzy. It was then that he knew for certain that he was going to fall. He forced himself to look away from the water. He focused on the deck instead. As he peered at the tiny figures so far below, a sickening feeling swept over him.

"I pray the Lord my soul to keep!" Digory cried, clutching the ropes for dear life. "I fear I can hold on no longer! Farewell, Cubby! Farewell!"

But he knew that no one could hear him, for he was now so high up in the rigging even the gulls were flying below him. Digory thought of Cubby and how terrible it would be to watch his brother die before his eyes. He thought of Aunt Alice and his cousins back home, who were depending on him. And he thought of his father, whom he'd so hoped to find. He would let them all down when he fell.

You never know when your hours will end, Jonathan Death had said. *You never know when the wheel will stop.*

"I pray my turn is not over yet," Digory whimpered as he leaned into the rope. But at that moment the wind turned and he was nearly thrown off the line. He gripped the ropes for dear life and continued to pull himself up.

"If you see me through this, Lord, I will give up teasing the twins for the rest of my days," he began to pray aloud. "And I'll tell no more tales. I'll make amends for all the wrong I've ever done, like the times I stole crabapples from Neddy Crumb's tree or the time Cubby and I dipped Zimmie's braids in tar. I'll not do that again. Strike me dead if I do, Lord."

The sails snapped loudly in the wind, sounding like the wrath of God in Digory's ears.

"And come Sundays I'll not hide down in Grundy's fish cellar," Digory cried, clutching the lines. "I'll come visit you instead, in your house, Lord, the way Aunt Alice is always after me to do. If you'll only help me to make this climb, I swear, I'll mend my ways. I swear I will," he whimpered, pitching from side to side.

As he prayed, he continued to grasp the rope in the battle for his life. And as he climbed, Digory heard his father's deep voice in his ear, saying, "Don't give up, Digory. Don't give up, son." As he listened to his father's words, Digory pushed with his legs, pushing through his dizziness and fear. He went up higher and higher. And then, as if by a miracle, he saw the wooden platform of the crow's nest.

With the rest of his strength, Digory willed his legs to continue to climb. Up and up he went. And finally, to his great relief, he was there, carefully slipping himself through the hole in the platform. With a shaky hand he grabbed hold of the railing.

Once on firm footing, he sat down to catch his breath and rest. As he leaned back against the platform walls, a surge of energy rushed through him.

"I did it!" he said weakly. "I did it!" He had saved Cubby and Fishbone. He had shown the sailor boy the stuff a Mousehole boy was made of.

When he had regained some of his strength he took a deep breath and began the long climb down. Inch by inch he made his way, as the shrieks of the wind lessened and the cries of the gulls filled his ears once more, until finally he felt the deck beneath his feet.

"Three cheers for the little landlubber!" a sailor shouted.

"Three cheers! Three cheers for the landlubber!" the other sailors cheered.

"Three cheers for Digory!" Cubby cried.

Much to Digory's delight, he collected his penny, his dog, and his brother's undying admiration.

CHAPTER XII: A Crate of Crows

That night, as the waves rocked him to sleep, Digory's nightmare returned. Once again he heard the sickening sounds of cracking wood as the ship's hull smashed against bare rock. He saw the deck split beneath him as water rushed into the boat. He looked up at the bow and once again saw the vacant stare of the wooden angel as her golden trumpet dipped down beneath the churning waves.

"Help me, Digory! Help me, son!" he heard his father cry as the black waves washed over him.

"No, Father! Don't leave me!" Digory cried, only to find a sailor boy shaking him awake.

"Captain's orders," the boy said, giving him one last shake. "You two are to get an early start polishing the brass down below." He snapped a rag in Digory's face.

Digory and Cubby jumped up and spent the rest of the morning shining brass in the captain's quarters. After that it was back to gutting fish on the deck.

"All right, me lovelies, time for your breakfast," a pigtailed sailor called as he placed a crate of noisy crows down beside them. Fishbone sniffed curiously and cocked his head to get a better look. He pounced forward, and Digory pulled him back.

The sailor lifted the cage onto a large coil of rope, out of Fishbone's reach. Then he pulled a handful of crumbs from his pocket and began to feed the birds.

"You'd have had yourself quite a swim if you'd fallen from that rigging, hey, mate?" he said, eyeing Digory. "I never did learn to swim meself," the sailor admitted.

"But you're on the water every day," Digory said. "What if the ship should go down?"

The sailor grimaced. "Bad luck to speak of such things on board. Besides, I wear this to protect me and bring me luck." He pointed to the gold earring he wore in his ear. "Most of me mates do as well, and when we meet our end, they can use the gold to pay for our funerals."

Digory stared at the sparkle of gold in the sailor's ear. What could really keep a man safe? he wondered. What could keep the sea from taking what she wanted?

"Is that why ships carry crows on board, to bring them luck?" Cubby asked, poking his fingers inside the crate.

"Crows bring more than luck," the sailor told him. "And you'd be wise to keep your fingers out of there."

"Well, I'd fancy me a parrot instead," Cubby said, pulling back his hand. "One with green feathers who knows lots of words. That way we could talk, him and me."

"Green feathers and talk won't get you home when you're lost at sea, mate," the sailor told him. "That's when you need a crow, for they can find land where a man cannot. Every ship I've ever sailed on has carried a crate of them. When a ship's lost her way at sea, all a sailor needs do is to set some crows free and follow which way they fly. They'll always head for land. You can count on it."

Digory wished they had some crows to help them find their father. He imagined opening the crate and following the black wings as they took to the sky. If only it could be that easy.

"Do you know of a boatswain by the name of Nicholas Beale?" he asked hopefully.

The sailor scratched his whiskered chin. "Can't say I do," he said.

"Our father's ship was the *Flying Cloud*. It was out of Plymouth and wrecked at Yarmouth," Digory pressed, "some six and twenty days ago."

The sailor scowled, sucking in his thin lips. "Oh, aye. I did hear of a ship going down at Yarmouth. But I heard nothing more."

Digory's face fell. "Do you know how to get to the alehouse in Plymouth?" he asked. "Our aunt sent us to look for the ship's posting there."

The sailor half smiled. "There's many an alehouse

in Plymouth Town. But the one you'll want is the King's Arms. From Sutton Harbor you'll see the old castle walls — the Barbican, they call it. When we dock, you make for the Barbican steps, and then get yourselves to Greyfriars Street, where you'll find the King's Arms. 'Tis where most Plymouth ships post their articles. They may have word of the *Flying Cloud* and her crew."

Digory saw a sad, faraway look come into the sailor's eyes then. "May you find the news you seek, lads," he said. "Our own coast has been our worst enemy, taking far too many good men already. God be thanked for the light on the Eddystone Reef. 'Twas a miracle that lighthouse ever got built."

The hair on Digory's neck stood up. "The Eddystone Reef, you say? 'Twas where my grandfather's boat went down." But before the sailor could respond, a loud shout punctured the air.

"Land ho!" one of the crew up in the rigging cried out.

"Plymouth!" shouted another.

The sailor collected his crate of crows and hurried across the deck. "Good luck with your search, lads," he called over his shoulder.

Digory nodded. But he knew they would need more than luck. He began a silent prayer, repeating it over and over to himself. *Let him be alive, Lord. Please let Father be alive.*

eave, heave!"

Kawk, kawk! Kawk!

"Mind that line!"

"All together now. Pull! Pull!" The timber of men's voices blended with the cries of the gulls and gannets overhead. The noise of pulleys and blocks sounded as Digory, Cubby, and Fishbone made their way down the ship's gangplank.

Digory gazed over the crowded dock. "We'll start by looking for the King's Arms. Stay close," he warned.

Unlike the small, quiet wharf back in Mousehole, Plymouth's dock was bustling with activity. Never in his life had Digory seen so many ships. Vessels of every size and design hugged her harbor. Dutch flute ships with their big round-nosed sterns sailed by, as well as sleek English brigantines with lion heads and lamps of brass. Exotic-looking Neapolitan ketches with triangular sails of white satin swayed in their docks beside men-of-war. And up and down the wharf, as far as he could see, men busily loaded or unloaded cargo.

Tea casks shot into barges. Barrels of whiskey rolled up and down planks. Bolts of lace shifted from shoulder to shoulder. Tattooed sailors with gold rings in their ears jostled beside blue-coated customs officers. Big-muscled coopers hammered iron hoops around barrels as sea captains counted out silver to their crews.

Digory wished he had his slate so he could stop and make some pictures, for everywhere he looked he saw amazing sights. While his eyes filled with images, his nose picked up the pungent scents of tobacco, vinegar, and rum that wafted off the hundreds of casks that lined the quay. Whiffs of bilgewater, sweat, sheepskins, and the putrid odors of horns and hides added to the stew. And everywhere was the powerful smell of tar.

When they found the thick granite Barbican steps, the three hurried up to the top. There the boys stopped to stare at the wide street filled with large houses and colorful shops.

"Look there!" Cubby cried. "'Tis a little house on wheels!"

Digory watched, amazed, as a small wooden house on giant wheels rolled by, pulled by two gray mares. A man sat on top, while another peered out from one of the house's small windows.

"What sort of contraption is that?" Cubby cried. "The world is far bigger than Mousehole. How will we ever find Father in a place so big?"

Though Digory's spirits sank at the daunting task before them, he clung to the hope that their father was somewhere close by. "If he is here, we shall find him," he said as confidently as he could.

But as they searched up and down the wide avenue, neither could read the painted signs that hung over the doorways.

"Pray, mistress, can you tell us the way to Greyfriars Street?" Digory finally asked a wrinkled old woman selling crabs at a crosswalk.

"Aye, m' dear, you must go down that street there and turn at the oyster stall," she said, pointing a gnarled finger. "Then follow the footpath to the sail shop and turn right, then another left. You'll find yourselves on Greyfriars Street, sure as you'll find good eating in a shell." She reached into her basket and pulled out a large crab, whose legs were still moving. "Only a half penny for the likes of you, dearie," she added with a toothless smile.

Digory shook his head no and thanked her. Then he tried following the old woman's directions, but soon they found themselves on the wrong footpath and completely lost. Fishbone stopped often to gnaw on something tasty in the gutter, a dirty heel of bread, a crusty fishtail, or a moldy piece of fat. And each time he would catch up to the boys, happily chewing his latest delicacy.

"Let us buy something to eat now," Cubby begged when they came upon a cart selling pasties and oysters for a penny.

Their mouths watered at the thought of food, and Digory couldn't wait to spend the penny he had won at such a price. But when he reached into his pocket, it was empty. The coin was gone! He quickly dug his hand into his other pocket, only to find it empty as well. And not only was his penny gone, but the watch was missing, too! What could have happened? It was then that he remembered how the sailor boy had leaned over him when he woke that morning.

"I've been robbed!" Digory cried. "The boy on the ship must have taken the penny and my timepiece while we slept!"

"Push off, you two," the man behind the cart growled. "I should 'ave known you little beggars hadn't any coin to spend. Push off, or I'll call the constable!"

Fishbone snarled and barked at the man while Digory sadly led him away, with Cubby close behind. They passed by a group of leathery-faced sailors toting trunks, rope, and tackle.

"Herring, mackerel, oysters 'ere!" a fish seller shouted from a doorstep.

"What will we do now?" Cubby asked when they came to a stop before an alley.

But there was nothing they could do. The money and the watch were gone, and so was the boat. The boys kept on walking, hunger gnawing at their bellies. Cubby picked up a piece of rotting cabbage from the gutter. He ripped a leaf off the cabbage and shoved it into his mouth. Then he pulled off another leaf and handed it to Digory.

Soon the two were competing with Fishbone, searching the gutter for anything they could find to eat, no matter how dirty or rotten. Pushing through the crowded cobblestone street, Digory stopped a man who was sweeping a footpath.

"Pardon, me, sir, but can you show me the way to Greyfriars Street and the King's Arms?" he asked.

"Why, you're standing on Greyfriars already, lad," the man told him. "And do you see the gold crown on the sign over the alehouse door at the corner? That's the King's Arms, right there."

Digory and Cubby thanked the man, then hurried down the street to the stone building with a large gold crown painted on its sign. Once outside the door, they heard the loud clatter of mugs and the voices of men singing and shouting from inside. Digory pressed his nose to a thick leaded-glass window. But the pane was so blackened with grime and smoke from within, he could not see inside.

He started for the door, but stopped suddenly as the contents of a chamber pot from a second-floor window came splashing down, missing them by inches. The sharp stink in the air made the boys gag. But more startling still was the familiar sound of a man's deep voice calling out a toast from within.

"To the captain's health! Raise your tankards, mates," the man shouted.

Digory and Cubby froze.

"That sounds like Father!" Cubby whispered.

"Aye!" Digory said, his heart pounding. He pushed the door open and stepped over the threshold.

Once inside the dark, smoky room, the three went from table to table. Digory searched the weathered faces of the men who slouched over pots of ale and puffed on long clay pipes. His ears pricked up at the voices of the drunken sailors, who shouted over their cards and then grew suddenly quiet at the clatter of the worn dice that rolled on the dirty stone floor. But their father was nowhere to be found. That is, until they heard his familiar voice call out once again. "And here's another to our good captain's health!"

Digory and Cubby made their way through the crowd until they came to a figure sitting at a table in a dark corner. Although his back was to them, Digory recognized his father's thick, dark curls and the familiar slump of his shoulders. All at once the boys rushed to his side.

"Father! Oh, Father!" Digory and Cubby cried together. "You're alive! You're really alive!"

CHAPTER XIV: Plaguey Little Wharf Rats

A hush fell over the room as the man turned around in his seat. But the face that stared back was not the face of their father. He wore a black patch over one eye, and his other good eye was brown. He had a big, blotchy nose and badly blackened teeth. This man was definitely *not* Nicholas Beale!

"Forgive us, sir," Digory pleaded as the man stared back at them. "We mistook you for our father."

An awkward silence followed, as all eyes turned on the three.

"A drink to all the sons I never knew I had," the man shouted. "Raise your tankards, mates! And raise 'em high!"

The room erupted into laughter and conversations resumed, along with the clatter of mugs and smoke billowing all around them. Cubby was so overcome with disappointment that he took no notice of where he was going. He stumbled over Fishbone and fell onto a game of tabletop ninepins. He landed with a crash on the hard stone floor.

"Watch out! You've spoiled our game!" a sailor shouted. Fishbone barked and Cubby grabbed hold of the table.

"The devil take you!" hollered another man.

"Out with you now and take your mangy mutt with you," the burly innkeeper, who was carrying a tray full of mugs, ordered. "Go on, get out!"

But Digory didn't move. "We were just looking for —"

The innkeeper put down his tray and grabbed Digory by his collar. "Take your search back out to the gutter where you came from." He lifted him up off his feet and began to shake him.

"Leave the boy be now," a voice interrupted.

Digory saw a handsome man standing beside them. He was not dressed like a seaman but rather like a gentleman, in a waistcoat made of fine fabric, with buttons of pewter. And though no wig covered his long dark hair, the silver buckles on his good leather boots told that he was a man of means.

"You really don't want to bother with this now, do you?" the gentleman said to the innkeeper. "Not when you've a customer wishing to buy a round for the whole house."

"The whole house?" the innkeeper repeated, dropping Digory to the floor.

The gentleman nodded. "Refill every tankard and put it on my bill," he ordered.

As the innkeeper hurried off to the bar, the stranger offered Digory his hand. It was not the weather-beaten grip of a seaman but the soft hand of a man whose palms had not been toughened from the living he made. Nor did the stranger carry the stink of his trade upon his clothes but instead smelled of deep earthen spices.

But there was something else about the man that set him apart. His voice was as rich and smooth as Devon cream. And a playful glint danced in his fierce black eyes, a playfulness not usually found in men who struggle with the sea for their very survival.

"Does your friend here have a name?" The stranger held out his hand to the dog, who was still cowering under the table.

"He's Fishbone," Digory said.

The stranger laughed heartily. "It suits him."

Digory was surprised to see that Fishbone, as if recognizing a friend, cautiously came forward and licked the gentleman's hand.

"And your father. I take it he's a seaman," the stranger said.

"Aye, sir, on the crew of *the Flying Cloud*." Digory rushed to tell all that had happened. How news had come that their father's ship had wrecked at Yarmouth. How Aunt Alice struggled to feed them. And how she told Digory to keep going should his father be lost. "So you see, sir," Digory concluded. "We must find our father right away, for we've nowhere to live until we find him."

The stranger rose from his seat and rapped on a mug with his spoon. "Who here knows of the *Flying Cloud* and her crew?" he called out.

All talking in the room ceased and only the clatter of mugs on tabletops could be heard.

"I do, sir," said a scar-faced sailor. "For she was one of our own. A Plymouth ship she was."

"Were there any survivors?" the gentleman asked.

"Nay, sir, not a one," another sailor answered sadly. "I lost me own brother in that wreck. Took the captain and his whole crew down."

Digory saw the panic in Cubby's eyes. "Could there be a mistake?" Digory asked. "Could some have survived?"

"Will Stillwagon was there," said another sailor. "He was in Yarmouth the night the *Flying Cloud* went down. He said the storm was so fierce that she slammed right into the rocks, splitting her hull clean open. They never had a chance."

The chatter and clatter rose once again.

"Henry!" a man called from across the room. "We need another for a game of whist."

The gentleman was hustled along to the card table as Digory and Cubby, dumbfounded by the news, were pushed through the crowded room to the door, with Fishbone following behind. Once outside, the big-muscled innkeeper appeared in the doorway, wielding a heather broom like a weapon.

"Off with you now, you plaguey little wharf rats," he shouted, bringing his stiff broom down on their heads, a bristle just missing Digory's eyes. Fishbone caught it on the nose and yelped.

"I'll give you worse the next time," the man threatened.

Digory grabbed hold of Cubby's arm and they scrambled down the street without looking back. They ducked into an alley and raced through a crowded crosswalk. They ran under the bloodied heads of sheep that hung from a butcher shop's awning and past baskets and crates filled with oysters and crabs. They darted up one muddied street and down another. Only when Digory tripped on a sleeping piglet did they finally stop. Cubby collapsed on a doorstep to catch his breath as the piglet went squealing loudly down an alley, and Digory sank down beside him.

Neither spoke for a long while.

"Digory," Cubby finally whispered, "I won't ever get my whistle from the other side of the world, will I?"

Digory hung his head and didn't answer.

"But Father promised me," Cubby said, his eyes filling with tears.

Digory thought of Aunt Alice, and how she'd said that promises were like piecrust and so easily broken. How right she had been! For hadn't their own mother promised to love them forever? Hadn't their father given them his word that he'd return? Even Aunt Alice had gone back on her promise to their father to look out for them.

A gull screeched from a nearby rooftop. A sheet of canvas snapped in the breeze beside a sail-shop door. Digory felt his own heart, brittle and broken, snapping into pieces. The hard Plymouth breeze stung his cheeks as it whipped across his face.

Cubby's little chest heaved with sobs he could no longer hold in. As Digory wrapped his arms around him, the two rocked back and forth. And as they rocked, Digory heard Aunt Alice's words in his head: "If you do not find your father, keep on going."

But where could they go? And who could they turn to for help? Digory could feel the fear rising inside of him like a wave swelling up and threatening to knock him down.

CHAPTER XV: The Jester of Littlebury

ometimes it takes hardship and misfortune to weave people and places together in just the right way. Sometimes it isn't until one is lost that the perfect path is found. Digory Beale did not know this yet, but he was about to find out.

As he and Cubby sat on a doorstep, two boys hurtled toward them. Their eyes were wild and desperate.

"Here, cockroach, catch! Have a little present!" one boy shouted as he shoved a large birdcage onto Cubby's lap and ran away. Stunned, Digory and Cubby stared down at the gilded cage and the large, beautiful bird inside of it.

"Scuppered again! Scuppered again!" the bird cried, flapping his brilliant blue wings.

"Thundering gales!" Cubby gasped. "'Tis a parrot!"

"It is indeed!" Digory said. "But what are we to do with it?"

"He said it was a present," said Cubby.

Both boys stared at the parrot. The bird stared back with its beady black eyes.

"Ain't he the most beautiful bird you've ever seen?" Cubby cried.

"But why would they give him to *us*?" Digory wondered out loud.

But before he could wonder too long, his question was answered.

"There they are, Constable!" a trim man with a face like a weasel shouted. "There's my parrot and the little thieves wot stole him from me!"

The next moment he snatched the birdcage from Cubby's lap. Meanwhile, the constable, a beefy-faced man in a blue coat, grabbed Digory by the arm and yanked him off the steps.

"The jig is up now," the constable growled. "You'll answer for this."

"But we've done you no wrong, sir," Digory protested.

"Why, you brassy little thief!" the man shouted, boxing his ears. "Dare you lie to the law after I've caught you with the stolen goods right in your hands? Give over your names. And be quick about it."

"Beale, sir. Digory and Cubby Beale, from the village of Mousehole," Digory told him. "But I pray you, sir —"

"Save your prayers for your maker," the constable snapped. "I dare say you'll be meeting him soon enough, for we'll not abide thievery in Plymouth Town. Many have swung for stealing less."

Digory's mind raced back to Ross's warning and the

story of the nine-year-old girl who lost her life for stealing a lace collar. He had meant to stay clear of trouble, but how was he to avoid it when trouble was thrown into their laps?

Before Digory could protest further, the constable called for some rope from a nearby shop. He quickly bound Digory's hands in front of him. Another rope was tied around his neck. Cubby was similarly trussed, and the two were pulled down the street for all to see and jeer at. The coarse rope cut into Digory's neck as he was jerked forward. Fishbone ran out from behind a stall and followed.

"What 'ave you there, constable?" called a man holding a long black eel over a barrel.

"Pair of thieves," the constable's deep voice boomed. "Beale's the name."

"Thieving Beale brats!" a woman hissed from an oyster stall.

Someone threw a rotten fish. It hit the side of Digory's head. His face burned with shame at the howls of laughter that followed and at hearing his family's name so disgraced.

"We are *not* thieves!" Digory cried as he stumbled forward. "On my honor, we are not. The boys you seek ran past us. You mistake us, sirs! You mistake us!"

"Save your lies for your trial," the bird seller shot back.

"But we are innocent!" Cubby protested.

"Oh, aye, 'tis what they all say," the constable said over his shoulder, "until they reach the gallows, that is. Then they sing a different tune. There's no better remedy for unloosening the truth than making the acquaintance of the hangman."

Digory could hardly believe what he was hearing. This day was even worse than his nightmare.

"And just what crime is it that warrants this meeting with a hangman?" someone shouted from the crowd. Digory instantly recognized the voice. It was the gentleman who had rescued them from the innkeeper at the King's Arms!

"Stealing, sir," the constable answered. "Caught the little rogues with the stolen goods on 'em."

"Thieving little vermin," the weasel-faced bird seller added, holding up the cage. "Lifted it from me cart while I was waiting on a customer."

"Refuse to admit their guilt," the constable continued. "Born and bred for the gallows, no doubt."

The gentleman glared at the constable. "You'd see them hanged for this minor business?"

"Just doing my duty, sir," the constable replied. "Protecting the good folk of Plymouth Town."

"What price?" the gentleman demanded, turning to the bird seller.

"Price?" repeated the bird seller, his weasel lips forming a greedy smile. "For both the bird and cage?"

"For the bird, the cage, and the boys' freedom," the gentleman said. "Drop your charges and I will purchase these goods for double their worth." He turned to the constable. "Is my proposal agreeable?"

The constable shrugged. "Seems foolish to bother with such rabble, sir, but then 'tis not for me to say. If the bird seller makes no complaint, then there can be no charge, though I'd feel uneasy releasing such rascals back onto the street."

"Release them into my custody then," the gentleman said. "And I shall vouch for their actions. I am leaving for Essex this day and will find work for them on my estate."

"And your name, sir?" the constable asked.

"Henry Winstanley, Squire."

"Oh, my word! Master Winstanley of Littlebury himself!" The constable bowed. "And a great honor it is to meet you, sir. Why, all of Plymouth is blessed by your work, and I'm most happy to help, I'm sure."

Digory stared at his rescuer. Why would this Squire Winstanley be willing to buy them their freedom?

"Double, you say?" the bird seller piped up. "Why, to be fair, the parrot is most rare. His wings are clipped and he makes fancy speech with little prompting." He shook the cage and the bird squawked loudly, "Nincompoop off the mizzen! Nincompoop off the mizzen!"

"Has a bit of a salty tongue on him," the bird seller said, his narrow eyes crinkling. "Spent a good deal of time at sea. Favored the mizzenmast, he did. But he can talk pretty when he wants to."

"How much?" Henry Winstanley snapped impatiently.

The bird seller sucked in his thin lips. "I should be giving him away if I let him go for less than six shillings, and you did say double."

"Twelve it is then. Now unbind them," Henry Winstanley ordered.

The constable hurried to untie Digory's hands. "You can count your lucky stars that the squire here 'as taken pity on your sorry souls. You're to be in his custody now. But if I hear that you've given him any trouble, any trouble at all, you'll soon find yourselves in the hemp necklace you were born to wear."

Digory brought his hand to his throat, for he knew the "hemp necklace" the constable spoke of was the hangman's noose.

"Into the custody of the Jester of Littlebury. Now there's a strange twist of fate for you," the bird seller muttered as he counted out his coins.

Digory stole a glance at his new master. Why had the bird seller called him a jester? And what did he mean by a "strange twist of fate"? As Digory pondered these words, Henry Winstanley's dark eyes caught his own and he smiled a most peculiar smile.

CHAPTER XVI: Off to Tend a Dragon

ell, Digory and Cubby Beale. So we meet again," Squire Winstanley declared, after the constable and the bird seller made their departure.

"We're most grateful, sir," Digory said. "They would have had our necks if you hadn't stopped them."

The squire frowned. "The hangman does a brisk enough business in this town, without having to service the likes of children." He held up the cage and silently studied the parrot. "And now that you are in my custody, I have but one rather important question to put to you, lads."

"I swear to you, sir," Digory blurted out. "We never stole a thing. On my honor we were mistook for two others."

"Well, I certainly hope you never stole a thing, for I'll have no truck with thieves and liars," the squire said sternly. "And if you are caught stealing so much as an apple, I'll be obliged to send you packing back to the constable. Are we clear on that?"

"Aye, sir," Digory and Cubby said at once.

"Good," said the squire, his expression softening and his dark eyes twinkling as he held up the cage before them. "Now my question for you is this. What in Zeus's name shall we call this parrot?"

"The parrot?" the boys repeated.

"Aye, for he will need to have a name if he's to join us on our journey." He handed Cubby the cage.

Cubby's face flushed with joy.

"Are we going to leave Plymouth?" Digory asked.

"Yes," answered the squire. "We leave for Essex within the hour. You can join my house staff there."

"Will we get to work on a fishing boat?" Cubby asked.

"Nay, for my house is inland, on the Coach Road, in the county of Essex," the squire replied. "It is a large house and there will be plenty of work for you there."

Unlike Cubby, Digory was relieved to hear that they were going inland, far from the sea.

"Mizzen!" Cubby suddenly cried out.

"Mizzen?" the squire repeated.

"The parrot," Cubby said, holding up the cage. "We could call him Mizzen!"

"A perfect choice." The squire laughed. And it was such a hearty and contagious laugh that the boys laughed right along with him.

Then the squire called to a stout fellow, who came huffing and puffing toward them. "Ah, Will, here you are at last."

A heavy load of ropes and pulleys was slung over each of the man's broad shoulders. He had a wide red face with muttonchop whiskers, a nose as big as a turnip, and large ears that curled like two cabbage leaves coming out of his head.

"What kept you, man?" the squire demanded.

"Sorry, Master Henry," the fellow wheezed. He stopped to shift the heavy loads of rope on his shoulders. "But I had a devil of a time getting those pulleys you wanted. Had to try three shops afore I found them at Tuttle's down by the wharf. And then they wanted double their worth."

"I declare, these West Countrymen drive a hard bargain," Master Henry said, shaking his head. "But your efforts will not be in vain, Will, for these pulleys will serve our dragon well."

The boys exchanged worried glances. A dragon? What could he possibly be talking about?

"These two lads are coming home with us," the squire announced. "Digory and Cubby Beale, this is my steward, Will Button. You will answer to him as well as to me."

"But, sir?" Will Button protested.

"See that two extra seats on the coach are reserved for them," the master said, handing him a small leather pouch. "And purchase some barley and seed for the parrot."

"But, sir, they smell like week-old fish," the steward complained, pulling a face. "And 'tis a long coach ride to Littlebury."

"Get them outside seats then," Master Henry ordered.

"But, sir . . ."

"No buts, Will," the squire said, holding up his hand to silence him. "You've said yourself we could use some extra hands in the workshop, tending to the dragon."

Once more Digory felt anxious. Master Henry seemed nice enough. But did he really expect the boys to tend to a dragon?

"As you wish, master. As you wish," Will Button finally said with a loud sigh. "Come along, lads, let's see about finding the coachman."

A short while later Digory and Cubby were taking their first ride in a horse-drawn coach. They took an outer seat, behind the cab, while Master Henry and Will Button sat inside it.

Though the road out of Plymouth was wider than the coast road, it was still poorly made, with deep ruts and rocks. The going was slow and bumpy. But the boys didn't care, for they were still marveling at the miracle of traveling without moving their feet.

Cubby put some of the seed Will Button had purchased into his hand, then opened Mizzen's cage. But suddenly the carriage lurched over a bump, and seed flew all around them.

"Cubby, watch out!" Digory cried. He feared that if they should displease the squire in anyway, they'd be sent back to Plymouth, where they'd probably be hung as thieves. At each stop Digory silently studied his new master. But the closer he looked, the more puzzled he became, for Henry Winstanley's expression seemed to change before him like quicksilver.

One minute he looked as grave as a preacher at a funeral and the next he appeared as carefree as a boy. His face was a riddle Digory could not unravel. The constable had said that everyone in Plymouth knew of Winstanley's work. But what sort of work did this odd gentleman do? And what kind of person kept a dragon?

Several hours later, they stopped at a stream to water the horses, and everyone got out to stretch their legs. "With these wretched roads, this coach moves as slow as if it were pulled by snails," Will Button grumbled. "We shall never make the inn in time for a plate and a pipe."

"Look there!" Cubby cried, pointing to a large wind-mill that stood on hill. Its large white sails turned slowly in the breeze.

"Ah, the power of the wind," Master Henry murmured. "I've toyed with the wind many times myself."

Digory was instantly intrigued. How could one toy with the wind? But the master got back into the cab without saying more.

"Scuppered again! Scuppered again!" Mizzen cried from his cage.

"He talked! He talked!" Cubby cried as he and Digory took their seats and the coachman cracked his whip.

"Scuppered again! Scuppered again!" Mizzen repeated as the coach slowly but surely carried them inland, far from the sight of the sea.

And again Digory was left to wonder just who this odd man was, who played with the wind and kept a dragon — and was taking them home to live with him!

CHAPTER XVII: Homesick

s they traveled farther inland, the air changed from the salty, seaweedy scent of home to the woodsy-sweet smell of earth, leaf, and flower. The rugged wildness of Cornwall dissolved into gentle green meadows dotted with sheep and cultivated fields, golden with wheat. The scents were heady and rich and new.

Granite and slate gave way to thatched cottages covered in red and creamy white roses. No poles of fish stood drying beside the doors nor brown nets hanging on fence posts. There was no ocean in sight, and that was some consolation to Digory. Maybe now his nightmares would go away.

But the farther they traveled from Plymouth, the sadder he became. Somehow, leaving the ocean and all he had ever known made him ache for his father all the more. Digory could only pray that this new master would be kind to them. For without their father, they had no one else to turn to. Their old life was gone now. They couldn't go back.

The coach ride from Plymouth to Littlebury seemed endless as long days on the road stretched before them.

Each night they stopped at a different inn. Though the boys slept on straw in the stable, Master Henry allowed them to take their meals with him and Will Button in the inn.

"Tonight we will stop at the Inn of the Crooked Crow," Master Henry said. It was the fourth day of their journey.

The boys were getting used to the stares of the inn-keepers, as it was most peculiar for a man of Master Henry's stature to share a table with his servants. Even so, Digory was amazed and delighted at the plentiful and delicious meals they shared each night.

The bread was made of wheat, not barley like the loaves Aunt Alice always baked back home. The ale was darker than the weak homemade brew they were used to drinking. Instead of pies filled with herring and pilchard fish, there were joints of mutton and beef. The two boys ate more meat in a few days than they'd eaten all year! It all tasted new and unusual to their Cornish tongues, but the brothers happily filled their bellies.

They arrived at the Crooked Crow well after the supper hour. The room was almost empty but for a few customers and the innkeeper, who agreed to serve the boys only after Master Henry bribed him with silver.

The inn's low oak beams and white cobbled walls made for a cozy change from the cold, damp outdoors. Fishbone settled down happily with a bone beside the hearth, while Digory breathed in the heavenly aroma of chestnuts that were roasting over the fire.

"Some may call you strange, Master Henry, but none can accuse you of being stingy," Will Button said as he shoveled a large piece of mutton pie into his mouth.

The glow from the hearth lit up Henry Winstanley's face, giving his dark eyes a golden glint. "They think me strange, do they, Button?" He took a drink from his tankard of ale. "And what do you boys think? Do you find me strange?"

Digory almost answered yes, but the truth was, he had never met anyone quite like Henry Winstanley before.

"Well, sir, I . . ." Digory began. But before he could finish, Master Henry reached into his waistcoat pocket. He pulled out a handful of powder and threw it onto the fire. There was crackling and a popping noise as the flames changed colors, from orange to bright blue, purple, and green! Digory and Cubby leaned forward in their seats as they watched the splendid explosion of light.

"So, Digory, you were saying?" Master Henry continued, as if changing the color of a fire was an everyday occurrence.

Digory was riveted by the colorful spectacle.

"What conjurer's trick is this that turns a flame's color?" a man at another table called out, his beard twitching as he gave Master Henry a sideways look. "Could it be black magic you practice, sir?"

"Nay, sir," Master Henry answered. "'Twas chemistry, not sorcery, I used. 'Twas simply the natural salts that acted on the fire."

"Begging your pardon, sir," Digory spoke up. "But this thing you call chemistry, is it what wizards use?"

"Nay," Master Henry said, shaking his head. "I promise you I'm no wizard. Just a dabbler in wonderment, you could say. And a bit of a bumbler, if you must know." He laughed out loud and rose from his chair. "Now I must search for a pipe and have a word with the innkeeper." He left the table and headed across the room.

"Don't let the master's carefree manner fool you," Will Button whispered to the boys. "There's no bumbling at all about Henry Winstanley. They say that fortune favors the bold, and that's just what he is. The boldest and most fortunate man I've ever known."

As they rose from their seats and were about to go off to bed, Will Button reached for the long leather tube that the master had left on the table.

"We don't want to leave this behind," he said, "or the master will have my head! He takes it with him always. It's filled with his plans and drawings."

Digory's eyes fell on the case. "What kinds of drawings does the master make?"

"I suppose you'll have to wait and see for yourselves," Will Button replied mysteriously. He pulled a short goose quill from his pocket and began to pick at the bits of mutton wedged in his teeth. "But I can tell you this, lads. Our Master Henry carries the sun in his pockets, he does indeed."

Digory didn't know how anyone could carry the sun in his pockets, but he hoped more than anything that he and Cubby could depend on the warmth of Master Henry's smile, for now he was their only hope for a home.

That night as the boys and their dog lay cuddled together in the stable's straw, Digory listened to the rain splashing on the thatch above. He thought about another rainy day back in Mousehole, when he and Cubby had helped their father to pull his thick brown nets from the boat and carry them home in the rain. He remembered how his father had thrown back his head and laughed as Digory and Cubby hopped over the puddles.

A wave of homesickness washed over Digory now as he recalled his father's voice, so strong and deep and comforting. He would give anything to hear that strong voice now. He closed his eyes and listened, but all he heard was the sound of the raindrops beating against the thatch.

"Why did you have to leave us?" he whispered through his tears. "Why? Why? Why?"

CHAPTER XVIII: Toadstools and Talking Swans

The next morning they left the inn under a sky that was washed gray and hung with sooty clouds. Though the road had fewer potholes, it was still slow going. Once they had to stop for quite some time to let a shepherd and his flock pass by: a great, moving sea of bleating black and white wool. Farther on they were delayed by a herd of cows being led across the road by two small girls. And there were times they had to stop just to let the horses rest and drink.

The weather turned wet. A fog set in so thick the coachman had to stop to light his lamps. By late afternoon, the boys sat huddled together to keep warm. Digory was glad to see a brightly lit building in the distance.

"Is it an inn, sir?" he asked as Master Henry leaned out of the coach window to look.

"Nay, 'tis my house," Master Henry told him. "We are home, lads. We are home!"

As the sun pushed away the clouds, Digory watched curiously as they came to a stop before a grand white house that was trimmed in blue and glittering gold. It was so dazzling, it hardly seemed real.

Compared to the small cottages back in Mousehole, this house was a palace. It had a grand entrance and many windows of different shapes, each sparkling with diamonds of leaded glass.

As his eyes traveled over the house, Digory's amazement only grew. For the front of the house was adorned with a large clock face. In the center of the roof stood an enormous lantern that blazed so brightly it took his breath away. Crowning the lantern was a golden weather vane with cutout shapes of a moon, sun, and stars.

"Why, there must be a hundred candles burning to make this light so bright," Cubby whispered.

"It's the most wondrous house I ever did see," Digory said. "The master must be richer than the king himself!"

"Welcome to the Magic House," Master Henry called out as he stepped from the coach.

Digory and Cubby jumped down to the ground with Fishbone bounding ahead, circling the bushes and happily sniffing the grass. Mizzen peered out with his beady black eyes as Cubby took his cage.

"Good day to you, Daniel," Master Henry called to a gray-whiskered man who stood at a turnstile at the front entrance. "What news, man?"

The old fellow stroked his thick beard. "Tsk, tsk,

tsk," he said. "Pesky problem with the tigers, sir. It's their tails. They've grown much too big."

"Seems we arrived home none too soon," Master Henry said. "We'll attend to the tigers right away."

"Did he say tigers?" Cubby whispered, tugging on Digory's sleeve.

"Yes, I think he did!" Digory whispered back. "Tigers with big tails!"

As the two continued their conversation, Digory and Cubby looked on with apprehension.

"Come along now, lads," Master Henry ordered as he dropped three coins into the turnstile's slot and the old man waved the little group through. Fishbone, wild from having to sit so long on the coach, circled three times around them, then took off across the lawn and into the garden.

"Fishbone! Come back, come back!" Digory called.

Before anyone could say anything, the boys chased Fishbone along a narrow brick path that went under an arbor of honeysuckle and around a high green hedge.

"You two had better stay out of trouble or you'll find yourselves packed off on the next coach back to Plymouth," Will Button warned.

At the end of the path, Digory and Cubby found themselves in a garden that was a riot of glistening color. Neither of them had ever seen such an extravagance.

Flowerbed after flowerbed spilled over with colorful blossoms. Each was laid out in a pleasing design around squares of brilliant green grass. There were brick paths and arbors heavy with roses in apricot, crimson, and gold. The heady perfume in the air left the boys dizzy with delight. Waves of lavender and spearmint added their spicy scent to the mix.

"Look there," Digory said, pointing to a miniature waterfall that emptied into a blue-tiled pool.

"And there," Cubby exclaimed as he pointed to a whimsical-looking blue windmill with brightly colored sails. The sound of an organ's cheerful music spilled out of the windmill's window.

"And there and there!" Mizzen repeated from his cage.

Digory was so taken with the magical garden that he almost tripped over Fishbone, who was backing out of a flowerbed.

"Stay, boy, stay," Digory called to him.

But Fishbone was intent on exploring and would not stay put long. He pawed the ground, sniffed around, and bounded across the lush grass. When he dove through a cutout door in the hedge, Digory and Cubby jumped up and took off after him. As they came out on the other side of the hedge, they found themselves in another, very different garden.

This one was a menagerie of gigantic green animals.

"Look! There's a tiger leaping through a hoop!" Digory cried. It was true — there were wild animals of all kinds. Monkeys dangled from trees and giant rabbits lounged on the grass. A fox dressed in a long coat and top hat seemed to be chasing a horse and rider!

"Why, they're all made of bushes!" Digory exclaimed as he reached out to touch the fox's green nose. He was about to take a step forward when he heard a loud *shoosh* and a fountain of emerald-colored water shot up before him. He and Cubby stumbled backward, only to find another fountain behind them. And suddenly there were jets of colored water shooting up all around!

They headed for a path that led to a small pond. As if in a dream, an elegant white swan glided effortlessly over the water. Two ducks quacked loudly from the edge of the pond.

"Is that all you can say, day after day? *Quack, quack, quack*? 'Tis ever so tiresome," the swan said irritably.

Digory stopped and stared. The swan was talking! Cubby was so startled by the swan's speech that he fell backward into a patch of giant toadstools. As Digory helped him to his feet, the toadstools broke into a chorus of giggles! Then Fishbone pounced on a toadstool and began to bark.

As startling as it all was, it was wonderful, too. For wherever they looked there was something to trick the mind and delight the eye.

"Ah, here you are," Will Button called, coming down the path. "Bring yourselves and your dog into the house now."

Digory and Cubby did as they were told and soon found themselves at the grand entrance to the house. There was an ugly green gargoyle affixed over the door that closed its eyes and stuck out its long green tongue.

"I'd rather stay outside," Cubby whispered, his voice quivering as he eyed the gargoyle.

"We've nothing to fear," Digory said, trying to sound brave. "Master Henry?" he called as he knocked on the door with the large brass knocker. "We are here, sir. We are here."

The doorknob slowly turned, and the door swung wide open by itself! And the boys took a deep breath and stepped inside.

CHAPTER XIX: The Magic House

Upon entering the house there was neither Master Henry to greet them nor a dragon to eat them. A footman appeared in full livery, with a white powdered wig and silver buckles on his polished black shoes. But it was not his fancy dress that caused Digory and Cubby to stare. It was his silver face — for he appeared to be made entirely of tin!

Digory smiled nervously as the footman bowed and extended a rigid arm. He then ushered them into an elegant drawing room, where he left them alone. Neither Digory nor Cubby had ever seen a room so clean, so bright, or so beautiful. Embroidered tapestries hung on the walls and sumptuous silks and satins covered the chairs and footstools. Large crystal vases held bouquets of flowers and sunlight streamed in through the many panes of the leaded glass windows. Strains of music sounded from a painted box on the mantel.

"What are you gaping at?" Cubby asked rudely.

Digory turned around with a start to find his brother talking to a small dirty-faced boy who looked so much like Cubby he could have been his twin.

"I said, What are you gaping at?" Cubby demanded. But the boy only answered with a scowl. "I'll give you my fist if you come any closer." He raised his fist in the air.

But this only seemed to anger the boy, who scowled and lifted his own fist at the very same time!

"Oh, so you want to wrestle, do you?" Cubby threatened. "Well, you will be sorry, for my brother here is the best wrestler in all of Mousehole. See how strong his arms are? Come show him, Digory. Show him your muscles." He reached over and pulled Digory closer, only to find the other boy had a friend as well!

Digory was about to speak to the boys when he suddenly noticed the cage in the smaller boy's hand and the blue parrot inside of it.

"Why, we're as witless as a couple of clams!" he said, reaching out to feel the smooth glass before them. "'Tis your own self you're picking a fight with, Cubby! See, there is Mizzen in his cage, and there is your black cap that Zimmie knit for you on your head. And that skinny fellow beside you is me!" Both boys were transfixed, never having seen themselves in a mirror before.

"I never knew I could look so fierce," Cubby said with a laugh.

Digory stuck out his tongue. They made faces and

danced around as their distorted images shifted and changed before them.

"Tar me, but . . . I'm growing fatter!" Cubby cried as he crouched down low.

"And I'm growing thin as a hay straw," Digory whooped as he stood on tiptoe.

When they grew tired of the funny looking glass, they moved along to another room. There, a long cherry-wood table was laid with silver and china. A loaf of bread sat on a silver platter. The bread began to move by itself! Before they could say a word, the loaf slowly marched across the table. The knife followed, and then the teacups!

"A loaf with a mind of its own," the master said as he stepped into the room. "What do you think of it, lads? I worked on that one for ages."

"Did you bake it with magic flour?" asked Cubby.

"It is not made of flour at all, but of clay," Master Henry explained. He rapped on the loaf with his knuckle. "When I said I worked on it, I meant that I worked on the mechanism to make it move. I thought you'd find it amusing. Now, I must call for our housekeeper to get you settled in," Master Henry said. "I will return shortly. So stay put, and whatever you do, don't touch anything."

Once Master Henry had left, Digory looked back at the table. The moving bread was still now, but he couldn't take his eyes off it. How had the master made it come alive? What did he mean by a mechanism? Digory was so lost in his thoughts, he didn't notice that Cubby had sat down on one of the master's thick-cushioned chairs with Mizzen's cage on his lap.

Just then two big wooden arms dropped down and wrapped around Cubby as the chair began to shudder and shake!

"Thunderin' gales, it's . . . we're moving!" Cubby cried. Indeed, the chair was moving on a track!

Digory started after it, but before he could reach the chair, the wall swung open and Cubby and Mizzen were whisked out of the house, screaming all the way!

"Abandon ship! Abandon ship!" Mizzen screeched.

"Help! Help!" Cubby cried.

Digory raced out of the opening after them only to find the chair speeding around a long loop of wooden tracks.

"We're going up!" Cubby cried. "And now down!" he screamed a minute later as the chair sped down another loopy rail high in the air and headed for the side garden.

"Hold on, Cubby!" Digory shouted.

"We're going into the water!" Cubby hollered, holding his hands over his eyes.

Even Digory winced, for it seemed as if the chair was headed straight for the duck pond below. But just as it was about to plunge into the water, the track swung sharply to the right of the pond. Then the chair slowed before coming to a stop.

Digory darted over to Cubby, who looked dazed and confused as giggles floated up from the toadstools around them.

"Good heavens, you've gone absolutely white!" a woman exclaimed as she came rushing toward them. "Whatever are you doing on the Mechanical Chair?"

"I didn't know w-w-what it was . . ." Cubby stammered.

"Excuse me for not introducing myself. I am the master's wife, Mistress Elizabeth," the woman said. "Are you quite all right?" She lifted up the wooden arms of the chair.

"Yes, I think so," Cubby said shakily.

"What's this? What's this?" Master Henry shouted, hurrying toward them. "I thought I told you two not to touch anything!"

Digory froze. "We meant no harm, sir," he said. "Please don't send us back to Plymouth."

"No one is sending anyone anywhere, but you could have been hurt," Mistress Elizabeth said, giving her husband a reproving look. "Henry, I insist you put a warning on this chair. They are not the first to take off on that thing."

"But no one has been hurt, as you can plainly see," Master Henry protested.

"He looks to be frightened out of his wits," Mistress Elizabeth declared.

"You've not been harmed, now have you, Cubby?" the master asked.

Cubby shook his head no.

"Would you fancy another ride?" asked the master.

"Aye, I would," Cubby said with a grin.

Master Henry smiled. "There, you see, Elizabeth? This new chair of mine will be more popular than any of our other attractions, I guarantee."

"Honestly, Henry, you should have warned them," Mistress Elizabeth said, shaking her head.

Henry turned back to the boys. "So what do you think of our Magic House?"

"Where did all these magic things come from?" Digory asked.

"From my husband's imagination," Mistress Elizabeth told them. "He has created all of the illusions in our house and garden. And you can only guess what life is like living with a gadgeteer!"

"And the tigers?" Digory asked.

Master Henry smiled wistfully. "Masterful creations of topiary, if I do say so myself."

"And the man with the face of tin?" asked Cubby.

"Ah, one of my personal favorites," Master Henry said.

"But don't he miss his skin, sir?" Cubby persisted.

The master and his wife both laughed. "Why, he never had skin to begin with, Cubby," Master Henry explained, "for I built him out of tin and nails. He's a mechanical man, you see."

So, Henry Winstanley was not only an artist but a gadgeteer and illusionist as well. All of the fantastical contraptions found in his Magic House were created simply to amuse. An entire house made just for fun! Digory was sure that it was the oddest, most interesting place in the world.

" 'Tis time you boys got settled in," Mistress Elizabeth said. "You'll find our housekeeper is made of flesh and bone and she doesn't like to be kept waiting."

Master Henry made a face and whispered out of the side of his mouth, "The woman is fiercer than any beast I know of."

"Henry! What a thing to say!" Mistress Elizabeth exclaimed. "Mrs. Huffy may be rather strict, but she is a fine housekeeper, and if the boys are to stay on here, they must obey her rules."

"A mechanical housekeeper," Master Henry murmured as he led the boys to the back of the house. "Hmmm. Now that would be interesting. . . ."

CHAPTER XX: The Huffy Bird

The kitchen was astonishingly clean and bright, from the snowy white cloths drying on a rack to the copper pots that hung gleaming over their heads. There was a heavenly aroma in the air, as a kettle of hot spiced cider simmered on the fire and a tray of gingerbread cooled beside the hearth.

Smoked meats hung from the ceiling and rows of polished silver plates lined the walls. Two girls in white aprons were busy rolling out dough on a board while a man stacked kindling in a corner. There were no hungry looks, no foul smells, and no dirty faces. Mrs. Huffy, the flesh-and-blood housekeeper, saw to that.

With her broad red face and her doughy fists planted on her ample hips, the housekeeper looked like a stout little general dressed in a mobcap and lace collar. She barked her commands to her small army of servants with a no-nonsense stare and a thick Irish brogue.

"May the heavenly saints preserve us!" Mrs. Huffy cried on seeing the mud-encrusted Beale boys and their pets before her. "What's that you're carrying in that cage, boy?"

"He's a ship's parrot," Cubby said proudly. "His name is Mizzen."

"I don't care if his name is King William," Mrs. Huffy huffed. "I'll not have filthy birds flying about my house or dogs running wild." She narrowed her eyes at the boys. "Why, sure if you're not carrying enough dirt on you to plant a row of cabbage! And you've the stink of a fishwife's bucket on you as well!" She held her nose as the entire kitchen staff turned to stare and sniff the air.

Digory shifted from one foot to the other as everyone's eyes settled upon him and Cubby. He'd given no thought to the dirt or stink on his clothes before. Back home in Mousehole the smell of fish was a good smell to have on you, for it meant food on your table and coins in your pocket. But not in this fancy inland place.

The housekeeper clapped her hands and called her troops to attention. Fishbone barked and Mizzen whistled as Mrs. Huffy introduced the boys to the staff, then ordered them all "Back to work!" A flurry of activity followed as Mrs. Huffy guided Digory and Cubby to the buttery, a tiny room off the kitchen where the house ale was stored.

"You'll sleep here," she said, pointing to an empty corner of the cold stone floor. "I'll have Tom fetch you some straw. And after you've bathed, you're to put on these." She handed them each a clean pair of trousers and a linen shirt. "You can thank your lucky stars that the master of this house insists that his servants not dress in rags."

Digory silently fingered the soft linen shirt in his hands, so unlike the rough, threadbare shirt he was wearing.

"Breeches without holes," Cubby whispered excitedly, holding up his new trousers.

"I'll not abide unruliness in this house," Mistress Huffy said sharply. "If I find you two stirring up trouble, you'll find trouble aplenty come back your way. Do you take my meaning?"

"Aye, mistress," Digory and Cubby answered in unison.

Mrs. Huffy ducked her head out the door. "Tom, Tom," she squawked. "Fetch us a tub of water and a hard-bristled brush."

"Why should we have to wash when we had a bath just last month?" Cubby whispered to Digory.

"We must do as she says," Digory whispered back.

"She's as sour as an old whortleberry," Cubby groaned.

"Shh . . ." Digory began, but it was too late.

"What was that you said, boy?" Mrs. Huffy demanded, spinning back around.

"Old whortleberry! Old whortleberry!" Mizzen squawked, mimicking Cubby's voice so perfectly, it took them all by surprise.

"Mizzen!" Cubby gasped. He turned to see the house-keeper's reddening face.

"I've got my eye on the two of you." Miss Huffy shook a doughy finger at them. "And I've just the remedy for dealing with unruly boys, mark my words, I do."

As Digory and Cubby suffered through their bath, they vowed to stay out of the horrid housekeeper's way.

"We must obey Mrs. Huffy if we're to stay on here. Do you understand, Cubby?" Digory said by the well house later that afternoon.

Cubby nodded as he pulled a few leaves from a shrub and fed them to Mizzen. "I just hope these greens don't give you wind," Cubby said to the bird, who was perched on his shoulder.

Digory laughed. "Whoever heard of a parrot with wind?"

"Old Tom Wisp, that's who," Cubby replied. "He told me how his parrot once had a terrible wind from eating too many greens."

Just then Mercy, the scullery maid, came trudging down the gravel path. She was a young, sad-faced girl, about Digory's age, with dark curls spilling out of an old, soiled white mobcap and a long, stained grayish apron. Her hands were rough and reddened from scrubbing the kitchen pots every day.

"Must be pleasant to rest while other folk toil," Mercy complained. "Cook never thinks to give me a rest." She lifted the heavy yoke from her shoulders and set the two buckets on the ground. She smiled as she reached out to pet Fishbone. It was then that Digory noticed her dimples and how her whole face lit up as she looked at their animals.

"Why, hello," she cooed, stroking Fishbone's head. "My name is Mercy. Do you have a name?"

"His name is Fishbone," Cubby told her.

"And your lovely little bird?"

"His name is Mizzen, and he ain't lovely at all," Cubby scoffed. "He's a ship's parrot."

As Mercy held her rough, reddened hand out to Mizzen, Digory picked out a piece of charcoal from one of her ash buckets. He silently began to draw on the white plaster wall of the well house behind them.

"I've never held a parrot," Mercy said with a sigh as Cubby coaxed Mizzen back onto his shoulder. "Won't you let me hold him?" she begged. "I'll be ever so careful. I promise I will."

Cubby put the parrot on Mercy's shoulder.

"You are so lucky to have pets," Mercy said.

"Aye," Cubby agreed.

As they talked, Digory sketched a picture of Fishbone and Mercy on the wall.

"Why, that's me!" Mercy cried.

"And a good likeness of Fishbone as well," Cubby added.

"I never know'd a boy who could draw so well." Mercy beamed. Then she lowered her voice to a whisper and looked around worriedly. "But you'd better wipe it clean before anyone sees it."

"I will," Digory said. But he kept on drawing. For once he started making pictures he didn't want to stop.

They sat and watched as Digory drew Mizzen wearing a tall hat and perched on a stoop. He added a well-fed lady parrot beside him, dressed in a mobcap and lace collar. When Mercy noticed she had an uncanny resemblance to Mrs. Huffy, the children roared with laugher.

"There's grumpy old Mizzen married to the plump Huffy Bird," Digory said. Mizzen spit out a wad of green leaf and walked down Mercy's arm.

"Oh, there's a pretty boy, pretty blue boy," Mercy cooed.

Mizzen rubbed his beak next to her cheek. "Pretty boy, pretty boy," he said.

Meanwhile, Digory kept drawing. He drew for the sheer pleasure of feeling the lines flow so effortlessly over the clean white surface of the wall. He decided to make a picture of the Magic House. He was just finishing adding the lantern when he heard Mercy exclaim, "Heavens! You've covered the entire wall! You've made everything look so real. Who showed you how to do that?"

"No one showed him," Cubby told her. "Digory always knew how to draw. Back home he drew pictures on walls all the time."

"You best clean it off now before Mrs. Huffy sees what you've done," Mercy warned. "Or she'll serve you up some of her special tonic."

"What's that?" Digory asked.

"It's a tonic that she buys from an old gypsy at the May Fair. A ground-ivy tincture mixed with a spoonful of cuttle-worm oil and a pinch of viper's flesh. 'Tis meant to cure boils, headache, and waywardness in children." Mercy made a face. "I never had it, but Ned, the stable boy, did. He said it was the most horrid stuff he'd ever tasted. If Mrs. Huffy were to see your Huffy Bird there, you'd be having a taste of it on your tongue, that's sure."

"Which of you had a hand in this?" a voice suddenly shouted from behind them.

Digory's breath stopped at the sound of the strong Irish lilt. He turned to find Mrs. Huffy behind them, her face boiling with rage!

"Sure if you're not doing the devil's business now!" the housekeeper cried as she surveyed the wall.

117

Cubby was suddenly stricken mute, while Mercy looked as if she'd just swallowed a cupful of ground-ivy tonic. Digory silently opened his fingers to let go of the charcoal behind his back. But as it hit the ground loudly, everyone turned to look.

And just when Digory thought things couldn't get any worse, Mizzen flew up onto Mrs. Huffy's mobcap, where he let out a manly "Clap on me hearties! Yo, ho, ho!" followed by a small, windy toot!

et this horrid bird off me!" Mrs. Huffy cried as Cubby sprang up to retrieve his pet. "Why, you wicked, wicked boy! You'll pay for spoiling the master's property with your filthy scribbling, you will."

"'Twas not him, but me," Digory told her. "I drew on the wall, but I never meant —"

"Oh, 'twas you, was it?" Mrs. Huffy flew around in a rage. "Proud of your sorry self, are you?" She dug her fingers into Digory's arm until he yelped. "Mercy, you get those buckets emptied and get back to your work. And you," she said, turning to Cubby, "you take that beastly bird out to the garden and out of my sight."

Cubby and Mercy did as they were told as Mrs. Huffy dragged Digory into the kitchen by his ear. Once there, she sat him down in a chair at the table and told him to wait. She bustled out of the kitchen but quickly returned with a dark green bottle and a large spoon in her hand.

"There we are now," she murmured as she poured the dark green liquid from the bottle into the spoon and headed toward Digory. "Sure if this isn't just the tonic to make a bad boy wish he'd never done wrong."

As Mrs. Huffy brought the spoon up to his lips, Digory leaned as far back in the chair as he could. An evil smell rose up from the spoon. "I never meant no harm," Digory pleaded. "Please don't make me drink that!"

But the housekeeper silenced him with a look so sharp, his voice was reduced to a whimper. "Be still!" she snapped. "The master takes you in off the streets and keeps your neck from the noose, and this is how you repay his kindness? By destroying his property? We'll see now if you don't get a bellyful of what's due you. Open your mouth now, you monster. Come on, boy, open your mouth!"

"No!" cried out Digory. "Please, no!"

She pressed the spoon against his tightly clamped closed lips just as Master Henry barged into the kitchen.

"What is going on here?" he demanded.

"This ill-bred Cornish urchin 'ere 'as taken to destroying your property, sir," the housekeeper replied, her big round cheeks puffing out. She took Digory by the elbow and dragged him back out to the well house wall, with the master following behind.

Digory lowered his head, too sick with regret to look the master in the eye.

"Just look at the mess he's made," Mrs. Huffy fumed. "This'll take hours to clean. He shall be punished, sir. Of that you can be sure." She waved the open bottle of tonic in the air, releasing a wave of stink.

Master Henry stared at the wall with astonishment. "My word," he said. "What is that horrid concoction?"

"'Tis a horrid thing he did," Mrs. Huffy answered.

But instead of agreeing with her, the master broke into a fit of giggles. "The boy has an unusual talent," he said when he regained his composure.

"Surely the boy must be punished," the housekeeper shrieked.

"You may leave us now, Mrs. Huffy," the master ordered. "I will take over from here."

"I'll scrub it off," Digory promised after she had gone. "I'm so terribly sorry, Master Henry. Please don't send me back to Plymouth to be hung."

Master Henry was silent for a long while as he studied Digory's drawings. "I must say your rendering of Mercy is quite fine," he declared. "And this bird looks an awful lot like our own Mrs. Huffy." First the master laughed out loud. Then they roared with laughter together. But the master's face grew serious. "You have an unusual gift for drawing, Digory." His voice crackled with excitement. "And I can help you to make the most of it."

"*Me*, sir? But how, sir?"

"By studying, by learning," Master Henry told him. "You have a talent, that's for sure."

Digory's ears burned to hear such praise.

"But talent isn't enough," Master Henry said. "First and foremost you must work hard and give your all. Learn to read and write."

Digory wrinkled his brow. "Our neighbor, Tristian Killigrew, used to say that words in a book could not bring the fish into his nets. He always caught more fish than anyone in the village."

"Your neighbor was a great fisherman, no doubt. Reading is very much like casting your nets, but the difference is that with books a man can feed his heart and mind as well as his belly. Reading will change your life."

He reached into his vest pocket. "Have you ever seen one of these before?" He pulled out a small, round instrument.

"Is it a timepiece?" Digory asked.

"Nay, it's a compass. And it is most handy for helping you find your way. But you must be able to read the letters to use it. See here," he said, pointing to one of the letters. "This E is for east. And when you traveled from your village to Plymouth you would have followed the arrow pointing to the E. If you were to return you'd follow the letter W for west."

"I did what my cousin told me and followed the sea," Digory said with a shrug.

Master Henry smiled. "And you found your way quite well."

"But I didn't find my father," Digory said sadly.

Master Henry put his hand on Digory's shoulder. "I too have lost those I've loved. It is not easy. But your father would want you to go forward and make the most of your life. You've traveled a long distance on your own. And if you were to learn to read and write, there's no telling how far you could go. Books can stir your imagination and open worlds to you as deep as the ocean."

"I hate the ocean," Digory said.

Master Henry's dark eyebrows furrowed. "Such talk from a seaman's son?"

Digory shrugged, embarrassed by his admission. "Cubby fancies himself a sailor one day, but not me."

"Ah, I see," Master Henry said. "Perhaps your talents are better suited for land. And that is why I want you to be my apprentice."

"Your apprentice, sir! Me, sir?"

"Aye, if it suits you." Master Henry smiled. "I need a boy who can use his hands as well as his wits in my workshop. And one day you may grow up to have a workshop of your own."

"But I am no highborn boy, sir," Digory said. "My father could never make more than his mark on a page."

"And my father was but a country bailiff," Master Henry told him. "Your future is your own, Digory Beale. Aim carefully toward what you believe in. Your future will be as radiant as you see it."

As radiant as you see it. The words hung in the still afternoon air as Digory watched a beam of sunlight bounce off the shiny brass compass.

he stars were now aligned for Digory Beale, and he could hardly believe his incredible change of fortune. Drawing lessons and an apprenticeship with the finest gadgeteer in all of England! And to think that only a few weeks ago he was sharing a two-room cottage with thirteen people.

Digory knew how luck could change as swiftly as the tides. It could sweep in and out of your life like the waves, rolling along the shore. It could carry you along on the current or pull you under. He wondered where it would take him next.

"You must have a tour of my workshop." Master Henry interrupted Digory's thoughts. He pulled a yellow silk handkerchief from his waistcoat pocket. "What say we have a race? The first one to reach the windmill shall be the winner." He waved the handkerchief in the air. "Are you ready?"

Digory had no time to answer, for no sooner had the handkerchief come down than Henry Winstanley bolted across the lawn toward the windmill. Digory tore after him and Fishbone and Cubby, upon seeing them in the distance, bounded after them to catch up. Soon Digory was speeding past his new master, sure that he would win the race. That is, until a large mechanical hand shot past him. The hand's long fingers grazed the windmill's door.

"I won!" shouted Master Henry.

How did he do that? Digory wondered, then turned to see what had happened. The metal hand was attached to an accordion-like arm that had shot out from Henry Winstanley's sleeve!

"Seems we have a winner!" Master Henry sang and waved his extended mechanical arm in the air. "Always expect the unexpected when you compete with a gadgeteer." His eyes twinkled mischievously as he pulled the arm back into his sleeve.

When Cubby and Fishbone caught up, the boys laughed merrily as the dog barked. "Come along now, lads. Off to the workshop we go."

As the little group walked through the garden, the toadstools giggled. Master Henry simply nodded and waved to them, as if giggling toadstools were an ordinary part of everyone's garden.

But it was the master's workshop that impressed Digory most. It was a large sunny room filled with contraptions made of wood, metal, and glass. Mechanical birds with feathers of indigo and gold flew on wires overhead, while miniature houses, palaces, and towers stood on pedestals. Large jars of paint pigments in midnight blue, canary yellow, and silver stood beside bottles of colored ink and mugs crammed with brushes of black sable and red fox hair.

Designs of domes, roofs, and gables were strewn across a drawing table. Leather-bound books spilled over shelves, and maps covered tabletops. As Digory's fingers grazed the edge of a stack of creamy white paper, his excitement mounted.

What must it be like to draw on such fine paper? How would it be to use those brilliant-colored pigments? How much fun it must be to create so many amazing, magical amusements.

It was all so exciting Digory hardly noticed that Cubby had wandered off on his own. That is, until he heard a cry from an adjoining room.

"Help me, Digory! Help me!"

Digory rushed through the rooms of the studio to find his brother, but stopped short when he saw Cubby on the back of a gigantic green dragon. It had silver-edged scales, a long spiky tail, and great plumes of smoke pouring out of its nostrils!

"Cubby! What are you doing up there?" Digory cried.

"I walked up the steps — but they disappeared!"

"I told you these two would be more trouble than they're worth," Will Button said as he and Master Henry rushed into the room. "If you'd like, master, I can pack them off on the next coach to Plymouth," he added.

"No, please, sir," Cubby begged, turning to Master Henry. "Don't send us back! We'll not cause any more trouble. I promise."

Master Henry silently scratched his chin. Then he walked up to the dragon and pulled a hidden lever from under its scales. The dragon's entire back opened up, revealing a set of stairs leading up to its head! "There's no harm done," Master Henry said as Cubby walked down the steps.

Cubby's chin wobbled. "I didn't know it was a dragon."

"You shan't be punished. In fact, you have just tested our newest amusement. I guess the surprise works," Master Henry said.

Cubby grinned. "Can I go up again?"

The two Beale brothers quickly learned that life in the Magic House was never dull. They also learned that if a Magic House was to remain magical, the amusements had to be kept in running order. The boys spent their days sweeping the workshop floor, tending the fire, and fetching tin, wood, and paint, and whatever else Master

Henry and Will Button required. There was always something old to repair or something new to help Master Henry build. The dragon's smoke machine needed adjusting on Monday. The Flying Chair needed oil and fine-tuning on Tuesday. Wednesday and Thursday were set aside to pad the new Perpetual Motion Machine, while Friday, work was to begin on a new clockwork ghost.

Days seemed to fly by as quickly as the colorful sails that spun on the musical windmill in the garden. Mizzen and Fishbone became the best of friends, with the bird often riding on Fishbone's head. Although Cubby tried to teach the parrot new words, "Blasted nincompoop!" seemed to be Mizzen's favorite expression.

Digory felt as if he was living in a happy dream filled with bright colors, smiling faces, and magical gadgets. There was the constant sound of giggling and gasping as visitors from all over the British Isles streamed through the Magic House and its gardens.

"Oohs" and "aahs" spilled out through the diamond-paned windows and from under the rose-covered arbors. Fun was the order of the day every day, and the Jester of Littlebury saw to it that *no one* left disappointed.

As busy as the master was keeping his fun house running, he kept his promise to give Digory his lessons.

Each morning Mistress Elizabeth set aside time to teach Digory and Cubby their letters. Cubby made a poor student, as he could not sit still. He spent most of his time staring off into space, blowing spit bubbles, and making burping noises.

But Digory took to his lessons like a fish to water. Within a few weeks, he was reading and writing sentences by himself! It was as if he had broken a secret code and he discovered buried treasure within every word he read.

But as much as he enjoyed reading, it was his drawing lessons with Master Henry that Digory loved best. The two would walk into the village with a satchel of notebooks under their arms and their pockets stuffed with charcoal and pencils. The master made each outing an adventure and always found the most interesting things to draw.

"Do you see those stone creatures on the church?" Master Henry pointed to the ugly gargoyles that stretched out their long necks below the church eves. "Try and capture them on your paper."

Digory quickly began to sketch a gargoyle in his notebook. "Why did they make them so ugly?" he asked.

"They're meant to keep away evil spirits," Master Henry told him. "Though it's a wonder they don't keep away the congregation. When I was a young boy, I used to stick out my tongue and throw stones at them whenever I could."

Digory smiled at the thought of the master misbehaving. "Did you ever get caught?"

"Oh, aye, and thrashed soundly for it by the vicar." Master Henry laughed.

Digory was stunned to hear that the master had been thrashed. "Did you yelp?"

"Loud enough to wake the dead in the churchyard," said Master Henry.

"I would probably yell just as loud as you," said Digory.

Master Henry looked at him thoughtfully. "I bet you would have," he said. "We two are alike, I daresay. I see much of myself in you, son."

Son. It was such a small word. And yet it echoed in Digory's ears like the roar of the ocean. With a pang of sadness, he was once again reminded of his father and how much he missed him, and he missed being someone's son. The master probably means nothing by it, he told himself. Yet he secretly longed to hear the word again.

As they continued to draw, Master Henry pointed out chimneys, rooflines, and steeples. He taught Digory how to look with an artist's eye, with all of his attention. It was a luxury that Digory had never imagined possible, a

131

time set aside just for picture making, with all of the fine paper and pencils he could ever want. It was always his favorite time of the day, and his admiration for Master Henry only grew.

Days turned into weeks and weeks into months. The spicy scent of lavender and roses in the gardens gave way to the smell of wood smoke and the sweet aroma of apples on the orchard floor. September passed and October arrived, and one morning Digory and Cubby awoke to find that a November frost had turned the garden into a glistening wonderland. The peaks of the Magic House shimmered and twinkled in the icy cold air.

As happy as Digory was in Littlebury, he and Cubby often talked about home.

"Sometimes I just wish we could go home and Father would be there waiting for us," Cubby whispered one night as they curled up together in the buttery.

Digory sighed as he stared into the darkness. He often longed for the same thing.

"I wish Father could have met Mizzen," Cubby said sadly. "He would have thought him a fine pet."

Digory nodded. "I wish Father could have heard me read. He would have been so proud."

They were quiet for a while as they thought about all the things their father would never know about them. Then

Digory and Cubby snuggled close in the straw. As Digory began to hum the old familiar tune that Father so often sang, Cubby joined in, their voices filling the darkness.

> *"Dance to your daddy,*
> *My little laddie.*
> *Dance to your daddy,*
> *My little man.*
> *Thou shall have a fish,*
> *Thou shall have a fin,*
> *Thou shall have a haddock,*
> *When the boat comes in."*

CHAPTER XXIII: Change and a Broken Teacup

igory's nightmare started as it always did, with the sickening crack of splintering wood and the sound of waves crashing over rocks.

Once again the black water rushed over the deck, seeping up his father's pant leg. All the while the sharp edges of the Eddystone rocks ripped into the ship's hull.

White-faced, his father stared at the gilded angel, but her wooden eyes were unmoved.

"She won't help you, Father!" Digory cried. "She can't save you!" But once again his words were lost in the roar of the storm as his father disappeared under the dark waves.

Digory awoke with a start. The memory of the ocean's sting was in his nose and throat, and his father's desperate face played and replayed in his mind all morning as he went about his chores in the sunny workshop. Even the sight of Mizzen riding on Fishbone's head and squawking "Blasted nincompoop!" could not cheer him up.

"What ails you, lad?" Master Henry finally asked, looking up from his drawing board. "You're not yourself today."

But before Digory could answer, someone pounded on the workshop door, then burst into the room. "I've come from Plymouth with a message for Squire Winstanley," said the man, who was covered from head to toe in dust from the road. Breathlessly he handed the master a scroll.

Master Henry unrolled the paper and read in silence, his face furrowed with worry.

"What's wrong, sir?" Digory asked.

"There is troubling news come from Plymouth," Master Henry said. "The teacups are falling from the keeper's shelves. The seas around the reef are . . ." His voice trailed off as he continued to read. "Run into my library, Digory," he ordered without looking up. "And fetch me my leather case. Hurry now, son!"

Digory tore out of the workshop and raced through the garden. He looked up to see the colorful sails of the windmill turning around and around in the strong breeze. The cheerful notes of the organ music filled the air. But something was wrong. What was in the letter? What did the master mean by *the keeper's shelves* and *the seas around the reef* ? What reef was he talking about?

Digory shuddered at the sight of the sky darkening overhead. He couldn't shake the feeling of foreboding. He had grown to love Master Henry and his Magic House and didn't want anything to change.

But change was already in the air. A sharp breeze was already bearing down on Essex, a breeze so strong it would rip three whirligigs from atop the Magic House roof that very night.

And far, far away, on the Eddystone Reef, the wind was also stirring. A gale blew so hard there, and the waves rose so high, that another teacup in the lighthouse keeper's kitchen went sliding from its shelf and onto the floor.

What Digory Beale could not know then was how broken teacups were about to alter his life forever.

CHAPTER XXIV: The Angel

he hemlock branches creaked and groaned in the wind, and the sky swelled with blackened clouds as Digory ran through the garden. When he reached the master's library, he was surprised to find the door was open. Digory had never before entered this part of the house, and as he hurried in, he longed to reach for the books that filled the master's shelves.

On an ordinary day, he would have stopped and stared and run his fingers over the thick leather spines. On an ordinary day, he would have opened the books, thrilled to be able to read what was in them. But he had no time for reading now as he searched the room for the master's case.

A sudden rumble of thunder made the thick window-panes rattle in their sills. The big library clock in the corner sounded with a loud *Bong! Bong! Bong!*

Digory flinched as lightning streaked across the darkening sky. He couldn't say why, but he had the uneasy feeling that someone was watching him. Then the door slammed shut, and it gave him such a fright that he cried out loud: "Who's there?"

Another loud *BOOM* of thunder clattered around him as the windows rattled and shook. Moments later, a flash of lightning revealed something across the room that chilled him to his very bones. It was the wooden wings, the golden trumpet, and the familiar ghostly stare!

"*You!*" he cried as the wooden angel of his nightmares stared back at him.

But how was this possible? How had this horrid creature of his nightmares gotten loose in his waking life? And what was she doing here in his beloved master's house?

As Digory steadied himself on the bookshelf, he heard footsteps coming toward the library. He was relieved when the master's face appeared in the glow of the candle he held.

"Whatever is the matter, Digory? You look as if you'd just seen a ghost."

"I think I have," Digory whispered, pointing across the room to the angel hanging on the wall. Her golden trumpet shimmered in the glow of candlelight. "That angel! Where did she come from?"

"Why? What do you know of her?"

Digory was barely able to speak. "She's the angel of death that I see in my nightmares. She's the angel my cousin told me was on my grandfather's ship, *the Constant*, when she went down on the Eddystone Reef."

Master Henry looked visibly shaken. "Your grand-father was on my ship?"

"Your ship?"

"Aye," Master Henry nodded. "For I owned the *Constant* and I designed this angel as her figurehead myself."

Digory sunk down to his knees. He could barely make out what he was hearing for the loud pounding of his heart. Master Henry had owned his grandfather's ship! The ship that had wrecked on the Eddystone Reef!

"I was in Plymouth when she went down," Master Henry continued. "She was returning from Malta, a vessel of two hundred tons, laden with currants and Muscadine wine. Seventy souls were aboard the night she foundered on the Eddystone, but all that came ashore were bits of broken wood and sail, some hogsheads of wine, and this . . . this angel." His voice choked with emotion.

"When they handed her to me, I carried her back down to the beach and looked out over the sea. It was then I made a vow to myself and to all the men who dared to brave that cruel reef that I would do whatever I could to light the Eddystone. And the angel became my touch-stone. I would look at her and remember to stay strong."

"You built the lighthouse?" Digory gasped.

"Aye, and it nearly ruined me seeing her built on those unforgiving rocks. Four of my workmen lost their lives.

The rest wanted to quit her dozens of times. In truth I nearly gave in to them myself."

"But you kept on going?"

Master Henry's eyes became intense. "I had to, for I knew that ships from all over England would come to count on my tower's light to guide them away from the reef. I could not let them down."

Digory followed him over to a small round table where a miniature lighthouse made of silver stood. Digory had never seen anything quite like it. It was such a graceful and fanciful tower, like something out of a fairytale.

"It is an exact replica of my Eddystone Light," Master Henry said proudly.

"If only there had been a lighthouse like this to save Father," Digory said.

Master Henry nodded, then continued. "The people of Plymouth presented this to me after the reef was lit. One part holds sugar and the other salt." He unscrewed the top half to show Digory the salt within.

Digory stepped closer to the table. "It's beautiful," he marveled.

"Beautiful and yet strong," Master Henry added. "For the Atlantic is a punishing companion."

"But weren't you afraid to build a lighthouse so far out into the sea and on top of those rocks?" Digory asked. "You could have drowned!"

The master smiled a sad smile. "It's a small risk to save many lives. Many called me reckless, but I had a dream to light the reef, and I had to see it through. It was not something I could have done halfway. *C'est tout ou rien.* It's all or nothing."

His words left Digory reeling. Was Master Henry reckless? Did he care more about the lives of others than his own? What if something was to happen to him? What would become of Digory and Cubby if they should lose the one person who cared most about them?

Then, as if he were reading Digory's mind, the master said, "My lighthouse keeper has informed me that the seas are higher than we expected this year. The tower is swaying and the teacups in his kitchen are falling from their shelves. I've no worries about the strength of my lighthouse. It's more than strong enough, but some reinforcements will put my keeper's mind at ease. I must leave tomorrow for the Eddystone."

"For the Eddystone?" Digory felt as if he had been knocked down by a wave and had all the air beaten out of him.

"Yes," said Master Henry. "And I'd like you and Cubby to come with me to Plymouth and help. There will be supplies to unload. You can stay at the inn until I return from the reef. The sea air will do you both good. Bring Mizzen along, and Fishbone, too."

Master Henry looked back at the broken angel. His dark eyes flashed and he smiled a bewitching smile. "It will be good to see my lighthouse again. Good to be on the Eddystone. You can't imagine the thrill of standing high up in the gallery and looking out over the waves."

Digory nodded numbly. But in his heart the panic was already rising. And in his mind he heard a small, frightened voice cry out:

"No! You mustn't go there! Not on the Eddystone Reef! Not there!"

CHAPTER XXV: To Plymouth

It took all morning to pack the carriage. The boys helped Will Button carry the large boxes of tools out from the workshop. Master Henry checked the list he held in his hand.

"We mustn't forget anything, Will," he said. "And be sure to count all of the tallows twice."

Will Button opened a box and began to count out loud while Master Henry explained to the boys how the lantern room, at the top of the lighthouse, was where all the candles would burn.

Digory tried to imagine himself high up in the lighthouse, but he instantly became sick to his stomach.

"The gales are strongest on the coast this time of year," Mistress Elizabeth said to the boys. "We keep these coats here for my nephews. They will you keep warm." She handed them each a wool jacket.

Cubby's face lit up as he slipped his arms into the thick woolen sleeves. Though the coat was big for his small frame, he was beside himself with pride. For neither he nor Digory had ever owned a coat.

"I ain't never taking it off," Cubby declared.

"Not even when you bathe?" Master Henry teased, and everyone laughed.

Digory buttoned his own coat. It was nearly a perfect fit, though it felt heavy on his shoulders, like armor. He knelt down beside Fishbone and scratched behind his ears as he listened to Mistress Elizabeth's voice above the wind.

"Why must you always put yourself in such danger, Henry?" she said. The fringe of her shawl whipped in the breeze. "Why not send someone else in your place?"

As Digory listened to her pleas, he recognized the fear and worry in her voice. He'd seen it often enough on the faces of the women who stood on Mousehole's wharf, saying their farewells to their husbands, knowing they might never return.

"Now, Elizabeth, we've been through this time and again," Master Henry said impatiently. "'Tis my lighthouse and my responsibility to see that the structure is sound. There are lives at stake. We shall return in time for Christmas, I give you my word."

"But can you not wait until the storm season is over?" his wife implored. "Why are the lives of others more important than your own?"

"If we wait much longer, the seas will be too high, and we won't be able to get out to the reef until spring," Master Henry explained. "I must repair any damage before then. I promise you there is nothing to worry about. I have built a strong tower and she will protect me."

Digory winced to hear this. How could he be so sure?

The argument was interrupted when a raven flew noisily from the branches of an old beech tree and startled the horses. Fishbone barked anxiously, and Mizzen squawked from his cage. Mistress Elizabeth let out a gasp as the others looked up to see the large black wings take to the sky. Everyone knew that a raven seen before a journey was a portent of bad luck. The group fell deadly silent.

"There now," Will Button finally said, trying to quiet the horses. "Best hurry, lads," he called as he helped Cubby into the carriage. "You wouldn't want the master to leave without you."

I wish he wouldn't leave at all, Digory thought as he took his place on the hard wooden seat beside Cubby. If only there was a way to talk him out of going to the Eddystone. But as Henry Winstanley cracked the whip on the horses' hindquarters, the carriage nearly flew down the bumpy Coach Road.

As Digory grew more worried, he turned around to look once again at the place he had grown to love. What if something terrible happened? What if they never returned? As the horses' hooves kicked up a cloud of dust behind them, Digory watched the Magic House, the windmill, and the gardens as if he was seeing them for the last time. With a shiver he faced forward.

"The wind is fierce today," Master Henry called out over the roar and rumble of the wheels. "But God willing, the weather will turn fair by the time we arrive in Plymouth."

Digory gritted his teeth and prayed it would be so.

"I've hired a crew of workmen to help with the repairs on the tower, and a boatman will take us out to the reef," the master went on. "James Bound is the best coxswain in all of Plymouth. He'll meet us at the White Owl Inn. I'd trust no other to navigate those rocks, should the sea prove rough going out."

Digory winced at the words *rocks*, *sea*, and *rough*. They were the very images of his worst nightmares.

Littlebury disappeared behind them as the carriage bumped and lurched along the rutted roads through one town after the next toward Plymouth.

"Sir," Cubby asked as the carriage rumbled through Sussex. "How did you get your lighthouse to stand on the rocks in the sea?"

Master Henry smiled broadly, thrilled to be telling his story to a captive audience. "It was a quite a feat, if I do say so myself," he began. "To the sailors of Devon, returning home past the Eddystone had proven a greater risk than sailing in the open sea. The currents obey no laws on that hellish reef. The swells are so great and the rocks so treacherous that over fifty ships a year were lost to her. For years sailors dreamed of marking the Eddystone, but no one dared try. It was far too dangerous."

A smile spread across Master Henry's face, and he threw back his shoulders proudly. "That is, until my workmen and I drove the first stake into that merciless rock."

Digory and Cubby listened with awe at the master's amazing story.

"I shall never forget that day," Master Henry went on, "when I stood up in the gallery and watched the very first ship to be guided by her light. It was one of the most thrilling days of my life."

"What happens if the candles should go out when you aren't there?" Cubby asked.

"There's a keeper," Master Henry told him. "It's a difficult job to fill, as few men are willing to brave living so far out to sea. But I pay a good wage, and George Connors has been out there for months now. He and his assistant are in need of some relief and a fresh supply of candles. I'll warrant they've grown weary of eating fish. Why, even Mrs. Huffy's special brew might tempt them now, hey, Digory?" He laughed his hearty laugh.

But Digory smiled uneasily. He couldn't stop worrying about the master going out to the Eddystone, out to that killer reef — even though he seemed so certain that his tower would keep him safe.

Each night of the journey, as they stayed in a different inn and supped on hearty meals, the master regaled the boys with his wonderful stories about his adventures at sea. Digory and Cubby agreed that no one told better stories than Master Henry. They especially loved the one about how he was kidnapped by the French and almost hanged. Digory wished his cousins back home could hear him, too.

Eight days after they had left Littlebury, the carriage finally turned the bend leading to the familiar wide streets. They were lined with houses and filled with the commotion of people, horses, carts, geese, and pigs. As the carriage wheels ground along through the gritty sand, the sharp tang of tar and the salty bite of the sea air returned.

Plymouth! They were back. Master Henry cracked the whip on the horses' flanks in his hurry to see his lighthouse.

"It smells like home," Cubby said with a wistful smile.

A fishmonger cried as a gull shrieked from a nearby roof-top. "Who will buy my cockles, whelks, and flounder?"

At Plymouth Hoe, the bluff that looked out on the water, the master pulled back the horses' reins and brought the carriage to a sudden stop. Then he jumped to the ground, tied up the horses to a post, and broke into a sprint. Digory and Cubby jumped out after him. Fishbone raced across the green until they came to the side of the bluff.

"There she is!" Master Henry cried, looking through his spyglass across the wide expanse of dark waters.

Digory squinted, trying to see across the waves. But he could see nothing on the watery horizon. Then Master Henry handed him the spyglass.

"See how proudly she stands," he said.

Digory held the glass to his eye. And there it was, in all its splendor, standing all alone in the waves. Master Henry's beautiful lighthouse! But as he eyed the tower's base, Digory's grip on the spyglass tightened. For the whimsical-looking tower was sitting on the deadliest rocks in all of England, the very rocks that had killed his grandfather and so many more.

"Let me see, let me see," Cubby pleaded, taking the spyglass.

Digory looked up at the darkening clouds that were gathering in the distance. He knew that such clouds did not bode well for sailors.

"I shall head out tomorrow on the first tide," Master Henry said, looking out over the water.

"But the clouds, master," Digory said, his eyes still fixed on the sky. "Do you not see how dark and heavy they are?"

"Aye," Master Henry agreed. "But see there," he said, pointing to some gleams of light peeking through the soot-colored sky. "The sun is trying to break through. I believe it will clear. But let us not tarry another second," he said. "We'll stable the horses and then sup at the inn. If I do not get some food in my belly, I shall be in the foulest of moods. I'll send word for the boatman to meet me there. I've much to do if I'm to set out for the Eddystone in the morning."

Digory was amazed by his master's optimism in the face of what he knew to be an oncoming storm. But the foul weather afoot only seemed to fuel Master Henry's desire to go out to the treacherous reef. "There is work to be done if my light is to stay lit," he said.

And like a small, helpless shell being swept along on a powerful wave, Digory's voice was silenced once again.

CHAPTER XXVI: Devil's Smiles

s the day went on, the weather worsened. That November evening saw Plymouth's harbor jammed with more vessels than she'd ever had to shelter. Hundreds of ships' masters were waiting for the gales and the rough seas to calm as their crews filled the town's taverns to near bursting.

By nightfall the weather had turned ugly with a cold drizzle and a biting wind off the ocean. The boys buttoned their coats tightly as Fishbone tried to shake himself dry under the inn's overhang. Digory looked up at the large sign that hung over the door. He thought about when he and Cubby were last in Plymouth, and how he wouldn't have been able to read the words on the sign: THE WHITE OWL INN. So much had changed since then. They had changed. And it was all because of Master Henry. If only he would stop now and let everything stay the way it was.

"What's the name of the inn?" Master Henry asked Cubby, pointing up to the sign.

Cubby concentrated hard as he tried to sound out the letters. "The Wh . . . wh . . . wh. . . ." He was about to give up when he noticed the picture of the white owl over the words.

"The White Owl Inn!" he said triumphantly.

"Very good," the master said with a wink, "though I think you might have cheated a little bit."

The sign flapped and clattered in the wind as Fishbone ran to the doorway for cover, his tail between his legs.

They all followed Master Henry inside the common room, where the smoky air was thick with the aroma of fish broth, wet wool, and Dutch tobacco. The steamy windows rose above a row of boots that stood drying before a roaring fire. Men sat five and six to a table, slurping their soup, smoking their pipes, and draining tankards of dark, foamy ale. They laughed at the sight of Mizzen riding atop Fishbone's head.

"*Mmmmm . . .*" Master Henry cooed to the plump inn-keeper's wife. "What is that delectable aroma that lingers in the air, Mistress Boothy?" He closed his eyes and inhaled delicately.

"Could be our cod broth or our leeky pasty, sir," she answered as she wiped down the wooden tabletop that was sticky with ale.

"Either that or it's the stink of old Bob Kibby's boots drying at the hearth," a sailor shouted from another table. The room erupted into laughter.

"If his boots smell that good, I may be tempted to eat them," Master Henry shot back. He turned to the innkeeper's wife. "Bring us three bowls of your broth, three pasties, and a loaf as well."

Minutes later, Digory and Cubby were warming their hands over the steaming soup set down before them.

"Mistress Boothy will see that you're both well fed until I return from the stone," Master Henry told the boys between mouthfuls of broth. "Digory, you're to keep an eye on Cubby. Try to keep him out of trouble."

Digory nodded and glanced at Cubby, who was trying to get Mizzen to perch on his soup bowl.

"James! James Bound!" Master Henry suddenly called out to a dark-bearded giant of a man who had walked into the inn. As the man drew closer, Digory noticed his powerful broad shoulders. They were the heavily muscled arms of a boatman.

"'Tis good to see you, Bound," Master Henry said, reaching out to shake his hand. "I trust you are well?"

The boatman nodded.

"Have you hired the workmen and secured the supply boat with the food stores and provisions?" Master Henry asked.

"Aye, I've enlisted two workmen to accompany us."

"Excellent," Master Henry exclaimed. "First thing

tomorrow I'll have the candles and the rest of the supplies brought to the boat. We'll need to make an early start."

Digory saw the boatman frown as he pulled his wet cap from his black curls, which were plastered to his head. "If the weather stays dirty, 'twould be best to wait."

"Nonsense," Master Henry said, pulling out an empty chair at the table. "We've gone out to the Stone in dirtier weather than this."

"'Tis storm season, sir," the boatman warned, taking a seat. "This is different."

"I understand your concern," Master Henry replied. "But the keepers will soon be out of candles and there are repairs on the tower that must be made. I have no choice."

"You can choose to stay alive," the boatman said darkly.

Digory flinched at the word *alive*, and he searched Master Henry's face to see if the boatman's ominous words had made some impression. But Henry Winstanley did not even blink as he lifted his tankard to his mouth and took a drink.

"I promised to keep my tower lit," he said firmly, setting his tankard back down on the table. "And I must keep my word. Lives will depend upon it."

The boatman spit onto the sand-covered floor. "A cautious man does not ignore the sky," he said.

Master Henry smiled a wry smile. "A cautious man would not have tried to put a light on the Eddystone in the first place. I'm surprised at you, Bound, wanting to hug the harbor like a yeoman."

The boatman bristled. "A yeoman, is it?" His voice boomed so loudly that the tables around them went suddenly quiet. He rose from his seat, his hulking frame towering over the table. Master Henry stood as well, and Digory was horrified to see that the big-muscled Cornishman was nearly a head taller than the master! The two men faced each other and a tense silence followed. Digory looked from one to the other, wondering who would strike the first blow.

"They do call me a jester," Master Henry finally said, his eyes suddenly playful. "But I know of no better seaman than you, James. If any man can get us to the Eddystone tomorrow, it is you. And that's no jest."

As the boatman's frown softened, Digory sank back, relieved, in his chair.

"You try a man's patience," Bound grumbled. "That you do, Master Winstanley. That you do."

"Winstanley?" a sailor at a nearby table repeated. "Would that be the Henry Winstanley who built the Eddystone Light?"

"The very same," the boatman replied, nodding to Master Henry.

"'Tis an honor to meet you, sir," the sailor said, tipping his wool cap to the master. "Your tower is a gift to all of us here. Why, your light steered our ship clear of the reef in the storm of ninety-nine. We'd be dead men now if not for the Eddystone Light."

"I'm glad to hear my beacon was a help," Master Henry said. "I'll be sure to tell the keepers when I see them on the reef tomorrow."

"Out to the Eddystone tomorrow morn?" a sea captain at a nearby table exclaimed. "But why risk making for those rocks in such a rough sea, man? Why not wait until she calms?"

Digory held his breath as a hush fell over the room. Everyone stopped to listen.

"I've not the luxury of waiting," Master Henry said, brushing away the captain's concern with a smile. "There are repairs that must be made at once, and the lantern room will be out of candles soon. I'll not see the reef go dark."

"What say you of the talk in the taverns that your tower is unsteady and may not stand another storm?" a man called from another table.

"Some say that no repairs will keep the tower standing in *these* seas," another added.

"I take no stock in rumors that roll off men's rum-soaked tongues, sir," Master Henry answered calmly. "There was talk that I would never get my tower built. And yet there she stands. In five years' time not one ship has been lost on that deadly reef, because of her light."

"Hear! Hear!" someone shouted.

"Hear! Hear!" cried another.

"To Henry Winstanley," everyone cried at once as they clapped their mugs together.

"Now I'll give you a rumor you can believe, lads," Master Henry called out excitedly over their cheers. "I built my light to withstand the fiercest seas. In truth I hope to be in my tower during the greatest storm that ever blew under the face of the heavens," he boasted.

Digory saw James Bound's face darken at this. "Have a care for what you wish for, sir," the boatman warned beneath his breath. "Have a care."

But his was not the only voice of concern. Soon other whispers circled around the room and Digory strained to listen.

"'Tis folly not to fear the sea."

"Lose your fear of the ocean and you lose your life."

But when Digory looked back at the master's face, he could see that these remarks did not dampen his spirits.

In fact, they seemed only to fuel Henry Winstanley's desire to remain steadfast, for the look of purpose never left his face, his brow never furrowed, and his voice remained confident and calm.

Later that night, in a corner room on the second floor of the White Owl Inn, Digory lay awake on a dirty straw mat. Beside him, his little brother and their dog were snoring loudly. But Digory could not sleep.

Instead he watched Master Henry across the room, stooped over a small wooden table strewn with papers and charts. The master was so intent on his work that he took no notice of the hot wax dripping from the candle onto the cuff of his sleeve. His passion was so powerful it was frightening.

Digory closed his eyes and listened to the wind as it whistled through the panes and rattled the roof tiles outside their window. He pulled up the covers around himself and Cubby. The blanket was damp with sea air and smelled of other men's sweat.

As the wind howled off the ocean, Digory's worries grew. Everyone was telling the master not to go. Could Master Henry be wrong in his judgment? Could tomorrow's sea be too fierce for the boatman and his oars?

Digory listened to the sound of rustling papers and Master Henry's muttering. The master finally gave up and closed his big notebook. "I've gone over every inch of my tower," Digory heard him whisper. "The rest is in the Lord's hands." There was silence, then a loud sigh.

Digory could keep silent no longer. He had to speak up. He mustered all of his courage. "My father could not read letters in books, but he could read the sky," Digory said from the darkness of his corner.

Master Henry turned with a startled look, as if he had forgotten there was anyone else in the room. The mournful creaks and groans of a vessel docked nearby pierced the silence that followed.

"And those rays of light through the clouds today?" Digory continued as the words poured out of him. "Sailors call them 'devil's smiles.' They are meant to tempt you. They are bad omens, sir. They spell bad weather, of that I'm sure."

He heard the master sigh again as he snuffed out the candle's flame. "Then God grant me the strength to withstand what I must face tomorrow," Master Henry said in the dark.

Digory turned his face to the wall. "Please, God, don't let him go," he whispered. "Please don't let him go."

CHAPTER XXVII: It's All or Nothing

Early the next morning, Master Henry awoke before sunrise. Digory saw him bent over his papers once more, working in the dim glow of the candlelight. Before he left, he handed Digory his leather case. "Keep this safe here in the room until I return."

Digory stood the case in the corner and asked if he and Cubby could see him off to the boat.

"You'll have to be quick about it," Master Henry said. "There's no time to lose."

With the pets left back in the room, the boys followed Master Henry down the inn's old winding stairway. Once outside, the little group hurried over the footpaths, which had become slick with mud and horse dung.

Along the way a cat screeched under a fishwife's broom. The groans of a sailor, sick from too much grog, echoed down an alley. A pig noisily rooted through some garbage strewn in a gutter. The wail of a baby sounded from an open window. Plymouth was awakening under a dark, threatening sky.

The boys trailed after Master Henry as he flew down the Barbican steps like a man possessed. He seemed oddly oblivious to the ominous skies overhead. His determination was unstoppable.

Digory and Cubby raced after him, their hair flying back, their feet covered with mud. The sound of the dark waves crashing on the sand echoed everywhere. They found the supply sloop crushed up against the smaller ketches that were seeking to wait out the weather. James Bound was talking to the two workmen he'd hired, but when he spotted Master Henry, he frowned.

"Is there a problem?" Master Henry demanded.

"Aye, there is," the boatman replied. "'Tis thieves, sir. They broke into the supply boat last night and took all of the candles. Every last box."

Master Henry's face paled. "But those were no ordinary candles!" he shouted. "Those ignorant fools do not even know what they've stolen! Those candles were specially made to my specifications. The wicks, the dimensions — all of them meant for my lantern! Without those candles the reef will go dark!"

"There's Mulgreeve's Wick and Flame, just off the steps near the fish market," Bound told him. "They sell to all the gentry in the fine houses. They're the best chandlers in Plymouth, but you'll pay London prices for their wax, to be sure. But 'twill most likely take a few days' time to make such large candles."

"Price is no object," Master Henry said with a wave of his hand. "But time is." He turned to Digory. "I must leave now or I'll not be able to get out to the reef today. And each day lost could cost us dearly in lives.

"Bound," Master Henry commanded. "Let's make for the lighthouse at once! Digory, you must find your way to the Wick and Flame and place an order for fifty candles. I shall write down the dimensions. Tell the chandler you need them right away. We only have enough light for three days at most. They are to be packed in boxes to stay dry." He reached into his coat and pulled out a leather pouch. "Here is enough silver to pay for them," he said, handing Digory the money. "That should be more than enough."

Master Henry squeezed Digory's arm. "Go now, and do not let anything stand in your way. These candles are a matter of life and death."

"Aye, sir," Digory said. "I'll go at once."

"Good. Have the chandler send word to you at the inn when the candles are finished. And be sure that you accompany them to the dock," Master Henry continued. "Do not let them out of your sight once there. I'll secure another boatman to take them out to the reef."

If only you would stay, Digory wanted to say. If only just this once, you would hug the harbor and stay here with us. But he knew such pleading would be useless. "I'll see the candles are made, sir," he said instead. "You have my promise."

And as soon as he said it, he thought of Aunt Alice's remark. This is one promise that won't be broken, he told himself. This is one promise that must be kept. Together he and Cubby made their way through the drizzly, dark morning in search of the bright lights of Mulgreeve's Wick and Flame.

CHAPTER XXVIII: If I Only Had a Boat

igory followed the boatman's directions to the shop near the fish market that was ablaze in the most beautiful candlelight he'd ever seen. He read the words painted over the door: MULGREEVE'S WICK AND FLAME.

He gave the shopkeeper the order for the candles and placed a fistful of silver on the counter.

"Your master is most generous," the man said, returning half the silver. "This is much more than sufficient." He readily agreed to have the candles made and delivered as quickly as he could.

Digory and Cubby spent the next two days in their room at the White Owl Inn, waiting restlessly for the candles. Time was running out. The weather worsened, rain fell steadily, and the winds blustered and roared. Finally, on the third day, a knock came at the door.

"Who's there?" Digory called.

"I've an order from the Wick and Flame waiting in my wagon for Digory Beale."

Everything was going just as the master had planned. The boys left their pets in the room and followed the delivery wagon down to the beach. Now all Digory had to do was to find the boatman and see that the candles were sent on their way.

But when they reached the dock, instead of the boatman there was a group of men waiting. Digory looked from one face to the next, waiting for one of them to come forward. But none did.

Instead, a young boy approached him. "Would you be Master Winstanley's apprentice?" he asked.

"Aye."

"I have a message for you from Dan Scully, the boatman your master hired. He regrets that he won't be taking his boat out today."

"What do you mean?" Digory asked in alarm. "These candles must be delivered at once!"

The boy shrugged. "Master Scully got in a brawl last night and bloodied his face and smashed up his arm pretty bad. He'll not be taking his boat out today or any time soon."

"But the candles!" Digory cried. "He must take the candles! Lives will be lost if we don't take them to the lighthouse right away, before it goes dark! They've gone three days now on only the few that still burn."

Digory turned to the group of boatmen. "Is there one of you to take Dan Scully's place and row these boxes out to the Eddystone?"

"Row out to the reef, now?" one of the men scoffed. "Under this sky? With a fog thick as pea soup coming on?"

"I doubt you'd find anyone fool enough to risk that," added another.

"But if the sky were to change, perhaps later in the day," Digory tried.

"'Tis more than a morning of hard weather you're looking at up there, lad," a boatman said, shaking his head. "And if you're to reach the Eddystone, you must leave now while the tide is high, or you'll never get out of the Sound and into the Channel."

Digory reached into his pocket and fingered the extra silver pieces that were left over from the candles. "I'm willing to pay a good price," he persisted.

"No amount of money could buy that kind of courage," one of the men said.

"Or that kind of folly," added another. "Only a fool would risk going out to the Eddystone in storm season."

"But what of the lighthouse?" Digory reminded them. "If we don't get the candles out there, the reef will be dark all winter."

"There's talk the lighthouse will not stand another storm anyway," someone said.

Fear shot through Digory as he listened to the whispers that followed. It wasn't just the lives of the sailors that were at risk. If anything happened to Master Henry, Digory didn't know what would become of him and his brother.

Digory stepped forward. "My master built a strong tower," he shouted. "It has tamed the reef the five years it has stood. Not one ship has gone down!"

"'Tis easy to talk of taming the waves when your feet are on the beach," a boatman answered.

Some of the men laughed at this remark.

"I would go out if I had a boat," Digory told them. "We can't stand by and let the reef go dark. What of all those who depend on the tower's light? Think of the many ships that will wreck without it. Will you stand by and do nothing?"

The men were suddenly silent. They turned their faces away, embarrassed.

"I cannot let Master Henry down," Digory said, digging the heel of his foot into the wet sand. "All of his hard work will be for naught this winter if his lighthouse goes dark. If I could find only one boatman willing."

"You have found him," a gravelly voice called. A boatman stepped forward. He was not a young man, for his face was as leathery and worn as that of an old sea turtle. And though his shoulders were still broad, his back was bent. He wore a seaman's black cap over his gray ponytail.

"Have you a boat?" Digory asked.

"Aye," the man replied. "But it will be hard going in this gale, and I'm not as young as I once was. I can get us into the Channel, but if there is trouble, I'll need someone to take the oars to get us to the reef."

Digory looked back at the other boatmen, hoping that one would step forward. But no one budged.

Digory's heart pounded. "I will go with you," he told the man.

"Digory, no!" Cubby cried, pulling on his sleeve. "You can't go. You can't! You can't!"

"I must," said Digory. "I promised Master Henry. I can't let him down."

"Then I'm going with you," Cubby insisted.

"You must stay here," Digory said firmly. "Mizzen and Fishbone are alone at the inn. And so is the master's case. You must stay here and watch them."

"If we're to catch the tide we best not delay," the man called as he headed for his boat.

"'Tis madness, Cobb," one of the other men called.

"Think what you're risking, man," another urged.

But the old boatman's wizened turtle face remained unmoved. "I've no wife nor kin left to tie me," he said. "And I've an old score to settle with the Eddystone meself."

"My master will pay you handsomely," Digory assured him.

"Keeping that devil rock lit will be payment enough," Cobb Tomlin said. He spit on the sand.

Digory and the chandler's boy helped him to load the boxes of candles into his boat. Then the boatman secured them with rope.

"You know what Father would say: ''Tis not a good day for putting into the water,'" Cubby whispered as he eyed Cobb Tomlin's old bruised hands that were now reaching for the oars.

A fierceness shone in Digory's eyes. "If only someone had lit a light for Father," he said. "Aunt Alice was wrong. Not all promises are meant to be broken. The master promised to keep the reef lit, and I gave him my word to help."

Cubby blinked back the tears that were coming. Then he pulled off his own old wool cap and gave it to Digory. "This will keep you warm," he said in a small voice.

Digory put Cubby's hat on his head and got into the boat. His stomach tightened into a knot as they pushed into the waves.

Digory turned to look back at Cubby. But the small figure in the big blue coat disappeared into the crowd that had gathered on the beach. For everyone had come to see the crazy old man and the foolhardy young boy who were setting out over the dark, choppy waters, heading straight for the hungry jaws of the Eddystone Reef.

CHAPTER XXIX: The Light

They were less than three hours out and well into the Channel when they caught the main tidal stream. Above the choppy water, the sky took on an evil hue. Digory felt the ice-cold spray on his cheeks as he stood portside, clinging for dear life to the sides of the boat. Digory imagined the look in the master's eyes, and the smile on his face when he presented him with the precious candles. But these thoughts were barely enough to hold back the seasickness that had overcome him.

"Keep your eyes on the horizon," Cobb Tomlin told him. " 'Twill quell your queasy stomach."

Though the horizon line was shrouded in fog, Digory kept searching for it. But the sound of the boat smashing against the waves awakened his fear and dread, as he was certain the churning waters would pull them under at any moment.

Digory looked at the old boatman, hoping for some reassuring words, but the man's face was set in stone as he concentrated on maneuvering the sails. The boat pitched and pulled over the dark waters, and Digory clung to the sides until his knuckles turned white. Hours passed slowly as Cobb Tomlin adjusted the helm to hold their course. Again Digory longed to hear some encouraging words about the rough seas and the fog that threatened to swallow them up. If only the boatman would say it would be all right, that he'd been through worse, and that he'd get them through this. But the boatman's set jaw invited no conversation.

The skies darkened and the angry, whitecapped seas rose and fell. Digory thought about Master Henry and the many times he'd made this journey. He shivered as the ocean's damp, icy breath seeped through his skin and clung to his face.

Digory's admiration for Master Henry only grew as he understood the dangers the master must have faced to build his lighthouse in the middle of the rough and wild ocean waters.

The air grew colder. The wind and water numbed his hands and face. The boat lurched up on a wave, splashing salty water into his mouth and eyes. Digory searched through the fog, praying for signs of the light, for without it, there was nothing to keep them from crashing into the rocks on the reef.

Then the wind shifted and a wave hit them broadside. With a loud *crack* the mainmast snapped and the sail fell with it! The boat tipped and tilted with each wave as

Digory clutched the side of the boat, his fingernails digging into the wood.

"Take to the oars," the old man shouted. "They're all we have left now."

As Digory picked up the oars, he tried to remember everything his father had taught him. How he must put his back into it and pull with his arms. How he must not fight the current or spend himself too fast. He rowed and rowed until finally the boat seemed to be back on keel. He kept on rowing. There was no chance of taking a rest as the salt stung his raw, bleeding fingers.

Hours passed, and the oars seemed so heavy Digory didn't think he could row another stroke. Where was the tower? Where was the light? Had they gone off course? Had the light gone out?

The old man searched for the lighthouse as well, but the fog that was rolling in grew thicker and thicker until it seemed they could gather it into their hands and eat it. Digory began to worry that they would crash into the reef. Was his nightmare coming true? Suddenly it was as if they had entered a netherworld, wrapped in a cocoon of heavy mist that would not let them go. Digory could barely make out old Cobb on the other side of the boat.

"What should we do?" he cried.

"Pray," the old man answered as the boat crashed into a wave.

Digory knew then that he had made a grave mistake. The other boatmen were right. They should have stayed on shore. He sat rigid with fear, straining to listen between the wind and the waves for what he most dreaded to hear: the loud crack of the boat's hull splitting upon the Eddystone rocks. But what came instead was another sound, one he had heard all of his life. It was the sound of a seaman's shanty.

"Oh! Give me a wet sheet,
A flowing sea . . .
And a wind that follows fast,
And fills the white and rustling sail
And bends the gallant mast . . . "

With his head thrown back, old Cobb Tomlin was singing in a deep, strong voice, a voice that carried over the sound of the waves.

Digory found his mouth opening as he continued to row. Then the words came tumbling out and he was singing, singing as loud as he could, singing through his fear:

"There's a tempest in yon horned moon
And lightning in yon cloud,
And hard the music, mariners,
The wind is piping loud.
The wind is piping loud, my boys!
The lightning flashes free,
While this hollow oak our palace is
Our heritage the sea!"

And just as the song drew to an end, a beam of white light shone through the fog.

"I see it! I see it!" Digory shouted. "I see it! God save us, Master Henry, I see your light!"

There it was! Glorious, glorious light! Rising out of the waves, the tower stood like some graceful, magical vision before them. Digory's fear of the reef was now replaced with awe, awe for the amazing little tower that stood so brazen and so beautiful upon the rocks, showering them with her light. Digory began to laugh and cry at once.

But as they drew closer to the lighthouse, the smile disappeared from his face. For many of the windows in the lantern room were smashed and broken. A wooden crane hung off the gallery, nearly split in two. The weather vane that crowned the tower was bent and dangling in the wind. But the most shocking sight of all was the large crack that was starting at the tower's base and snaking up her side like a large, gaping wound.

"May the heavens protect us," Cobb Tomlin cried in a shaky voice. "She looks as if she's ready to fall! Why, she's no better than a death trap now!"

It was then that the blackened sky opened up and sheets of rain began to whip across the deck. The old boatman quickly regained his composure and took the oars from Digory. Whatever courage they had, they needed an infinite amount more. Not only were they heading for a battered "death trap" of a lighthouse in a full-blown storm, but they were about to row the boat into the angry currents of the Eddystone Reef — the vicious reef that had taken his own grandfather's life. Could a boy and an old boatman alone do what hundreds of sailors could not?

White-knuckled, Digory clung to the side of the boat as Cobb Tomlin fought to keep them on course through the churning seas. Even the old boatman looked terrified when a mountain of water swelled underneath them and the boat stood on her stern. The boxes of candles strained against the ropes. They were caught in a cross sea! The stern rose and fell, crashing down with a wallop.

Digory's stomach lurched each time a wave tossed them up into the air and slapped them back down on the water, and he fought the nausea that overtook him. The winds shrieked and the rains beat down upon them as they inched closer and closer to the jagged red gneiss rocks that jutted up from the water below the lighthouse. Digory held fast to the sides that were icy cold and slippery with rain. Then, as if a guardian angel had taken them under her wing, a man appeared at the light-house door. Digory barely recognized the master as the wind whipped his long, dark hair around his head. The very sight of him alone on that rock in that ferocious sea set Digory in a panic. Master Henry made his way, slipping and sliding, down the steps that were cut into the rocks. Two men followed.

"Come on, old girl, you can do it," Cobb Tomlin called out to the boat as he skillfully steered her to the ledge landing. And then they were there.

Master Henry threw Digory a rope and rushed to help him onto the steps. Cobb Tomlin tied down the boat while two workmen quickly unloaded the boxes of candles. The wind was so strong Digory had to fight to keep his grip on the rope as he let out a length to Cobb. Together they managed to make their way up to the lighthouse door as Master Henry guided them in.

Once inside the tower's circular chamber, they were met by the two bearded keepers, Connors and Matthews. James Bound helped Cobb Tomlin to a chair. Digory blinked as his eyes focused on the painted walls and fanciful gilded woodwork of the candlelit room. A spiral staircase with cherrywood railings rose from the center of the floor. But no amount of ornament could disguise the strong stink of seaweed and brine that was everywhere.

Master Henry gripped Digory's shoulders. "My God, Digory, what are you doing out here? You should not have come! You should never have come!"

"I brought your candles, sir," Digory said, startled by the change in the master's face, which had always looked so calm and confident but was now drawn with worry.

Digory watched as the door blew open and the wind tore in, nearly pulling the door from its hinges. The two workmen appeared with the candle boxes on their shoulders.

"Oh, thank the Lord," Master Henry said. "We are down to the wicks. Get them up to the lantern room at once!" He turned back to Digory. "I never meant for you to bring them out yourself."

"There was no one else," Digory told him.

"What good are candles now?" Connors said darkly. "The boy risked his life for naught."

"Not for naught," Master Henry shouted, his voice trembling. "These candles will keep her lit."

"If the seas are rising high enough to take out her lantern windows, what's to keep the waves from taking the whole bloody lighthouse down?" the keeper shot back.

"We don't know it was waves that took out the glass," Master Henry countered. "It could have been gulls."

"And what of the crack in her side?" the other keeper asked. "Did a gull do that?"

Digory stole a panicky look around the room.

"We've the tools to repair the damage done," Master Henry reminded them, his voice rising. "With luck the storm will pass and we'll be home in five days' time."

"You wish us to gamble our lives on luck?" Connors said, shaking his head. "I've worked as your keeper these many months now, but I'll not die for the sake of a light. I say we leave her now."

"You've done a fine job, Connors. And I thank you for that. But if we do not repair the tower now, 'twill not last another season." Master Henry tried once more. "Ships will go down. Lives will be lost."

"But surely you can see that the lighthouse is in no condition to go through another storm," James Bound spoke up.

"We've had waves come over the lantern, more than eighty feet high!" Connors burst out. "'Tis only a matter of time before she is taken down."

"Nay, she'll hold," Master Henry said stubbornly, running his hand over the mortared walls. "And I shall stay here to keep the light and to make repairs. But I will need help. I will triple any man's wages who will stay on." He pulled a handful of coins from his pocket and threw them on a table. "Who will stay and take this silver?"

No one moved.

"No amount of silver could tempt me to stay in this death trap," a workman said.

"Nor I," said another.

"I will stay with you, sir," Digory said.

"You cowards!" Master Henry shouted as he scooped the coins back up. "Go, then, but when you scurry back to your houses tonight, safe on shore, how will you look your wives in the eye, knowing that one boy was more fearless than the three of you put together?" He turned to Digory. "Come, lad, we've candles to light."

With his heart pounding, Digory followed the master to the staircase. If only he felt as fearless as Master Henry thought him to be. If only he could keep his teeth from chattering.

"A year's wages," one of the workmen called after them. "I'll stay for a year's worth of wages."

"A year's wages it is," Master Henry said. "Carry up the boxes and be quick about it. Each candle will need to be replaced." He took a rush lamp from the table.

Digory followed the master up the dark circular stairwell past a richly decorated bedchamber with lustrous sky-blue walls trimmed with gilded woodwork. The chamber's windows were covered with heavy wooden shutters that shook and rattled as if some angry giant were trying to get in.

"There, you see," Master Henry said, smiling triumphantly at the cozy room with its neatly made bed. "This chamber is as sound as the day it was built. You'll get as good a night's sleep here as in any lodging on Greyfriars Street."

Digory nodded, though he knew he'd never sleep a wink with the howl of the wind rattling those shutters and the sounds of the waves pounding against the tower walls. They left the bedchamber and continued up the circular stairway, around and around, coming out to a handsome stateroom with high plastered ceilings.

But as the master raised his lamp higher, they could also see spidery veins of cracks spreading into wider fissures along the ceiling. Not only that, but they saw two chairs whose fine burgundy cushions were covered with a white plaster dust. Large chunks of plaster had fallen from the walls and now littered the room. A crystal wine decanter lay shattered into a thousand pieces on the floor.

Master Henry's silence was almost as loud as the wind that shrieked behind the shuttered windows. He set his lamp down on a table. "There must be something I can do," he said aloud. "There must be some way to secure her."

A sudden crash of breaking glass sounded from above, followed by a ghostly whistle of wind.

"Good God, the lantern!" Master Henry cried as he raced out of the chamber with Digory following behind.

When they reached the open-air gallery, a blast of wind and rain put out their lamp and drove them back to the stairwell. The wind shrieked louder and louder as they rose, until they finally reached the lantern room.

Digory stumbled back, blinking at the brightness. As his eyes adjusted to the glare, he was stunned by the sight of the magnificent glass lamp hanging from the center of the ceiling, ablaze in golden light. Sixty giant tallow candles flickered around the room. Digory could see that most of them were burned down to their wicks. And one by one, the candles went dark.

"We came none too soon!" Master Henry cried out. "Hurry, Digory, take this lamp and help me to light the new candles!" He lit another rush lamp and handed it to Digory.

Candle by candle, Master Henry and Digory lit the lantern to the crash of the waves and howls of the wind all around them. And as they lit one after the other, Digory felt the brightness of all that golden light to his very bones. He and the master had done it. They had kept the reef lit!

CHAPTER XXXI: C'est Tout ou Rien

igory pressed his nose to a window in the lantern room. The waves were monstrous, and the ocean seemed to rise all around them. It was a terrifying sight, yet he couldn't look away. Then something odd appeared: the flash of white sails coming out of the fog, dipping and diving through the choppy black waters. A ship!

"Look, master!" Digory cried.

"By God, they see our light!" Master Henry said. "And it's guiding them away from the rocks!"

The wind shrieked, and the tower seemed to sway. Digory looked at Master Henry, who was standing there beside him in all that beautiful golden light. If only the storm would stop. But the constant rattling of glass grew louder.

"These blasted gales," Master Henry said, inspecting a crack in a window. "It'll take weeks to secure these things."

"The keeper thinks it unwise to stay," Digory spoke up. "He says the damage to the tower is too great. Please, sir, please won't you think about leaving with the others?"

Master Henry looked pained. "There are repairs that need to be made if this tower is to continue to stand. I will not leave her now."

The sound of footsteps echoed up the stairs. Moments later, the keeper appeared at the door. "The boatman is anxious to cast off, sir," he said as he entered the chamber.

"I understand, Connors, but where is the log I instructed you to keep?" Master Henry asked, ignoring the nervous timber in the man's voice.

"Here, sir," the keeper answered, reaching for a large book on a shelf. "I've taken notes on the weather and the waves, just as you requested."

"Excellent. Now if you would answer some other questions I have for you, it will help with the repairs," Master Henry said, paging through the book.

"But the storm, sir . . ." The keeper broke in, his blue eyes pleading. "There is no time. . . ."

"Yes, yes, I shall not keep you but a few moments longer," Master Henry said. Then he turned to Digory. "Go down and tell the boatman that Mr. Connors will be there presently."

Digory took the lamp and headed back down the dark stairwell alone. He shuddered at the unearthly howls of the wind. He had grown up by the sea and was used to the strong winter gales, but this storm's fury was unlike anything he'd ever heard before. At the bottom chamber he found James Bound and one of the workmen talking in hushed whispers.

"Listen to it," the workman said. "It sounds as if it's come straight from the devil's mouth! He's mad to stay. Can you not reason with him?"

But Bound shook his head. "I know Master Winstanley well enough by now. He'll not be persuaded to leave. And in truth, 'twill be a miracle if any of us makes it back in this storm."

"I'll take my chances with you and your boat," the man told him. Digory could see the fear in his eyes.

"We'd better leave now, for the storm is worsening," James Bound called to Master Henry, who was coming down the stairs.

There was an awkward silence. Everyone knew the danger that lay ahead for those leaving as well as those staying behind. Master Henry reached out to shake the keeper's hand. "Godspeed, Connors," he said. "You served the light well."

He turned to the boatman next. "I owe you much more than the silver I've paid you, James. When I get back to the White Owl I shall toast you properly." He held out his hand to him.

"I look forward to it, sir." The boatman nodded.

As they shook hands, the two men looked each other in the eye, knowing full well they might never see each other alive again. "See that the boy returns safely," Master Henry added, motioning to Digory.

"Me, sir?" Digory gasped.

"Aye, lad, for there's been a change of plan," Master Henry told him. "You're to return to shore."

"Without you?" Digory cried. "But you need me here. You said so yourself. We must make the repairs."

Master Henry smiled. "I'm afraid I will have to manage without you. But there is something else that you can help me with. That leather case of mine . . ."

"It's safe at the inn with Cubby," Digory told him.

"Good." The master nodded wearily. "You must see that it gets back home, for it holds important documents that mustn't be lost under any circumstances. You're to keep the coin that's inside for the coach ride back to Littlebury."

"But, sir," Digory pleaded, his heart breaking. "Won't you come back to shore with us? Please, sir. I beg you not to stay."

"Be a good lad and do as I ask," Master Henry said gently but firmly. "You've done a man's job already, bringing out the candles. But I must finish what I've begun. The lighthouse must be saved."

"Then let me stay here with you," Digory said, the tears spilling down his face. "Don't make me go without you. Please, sir, please don't make me go!"

The boatman opened the tower door and the wind tore in.

"Will you not change your mind and come with us, sir?" Connors begged one last time.

"Nay," Master Henry replied. "For I've a job to do and I must stay and finish it all the way. *C'est tout ou rien.*"

"French, sir?" The keeper frowned. "Don't understand a word of it," he muttered as he hurried for the door.

"You'll have to ask my apprentice someday," Master Henry called after him.

Digory flung himself into the master's arms and Master Henry hugged him tightly one last time.

"Please come back to the Magic House with me!" Digory sobbed.

"Don't you worry, son," Master Henry told him. "I promised Mistress Elizabeth that I'd be back by Christmas, and, God willing, I shall keep my word. We'll have us a grand feast then, hey?" The wind shrieked and there was another sound of breaking glass from above. Master Henry squeezed Digory's shoulder. "Go on now, the boatman is waiting."

*   *   *

The voyage back to Plymouth was a raging blur of crashing waves, howling winds, and thunderous skies. It was as if all the furies of nature had joined forces to wreak havoc along the English coast. Miraculously, they managed to stay on course for hours. But as they neared the shore a wave hit them broadside, and Digory saw James Bound fall overboard!

Thunder crashed overhead, while a loud creaking and cracking sounded from below. Digory screamed as the boards beneath his feet split apart and the icy water rushed up his legs. Suddenly he was thrashing and flailing to stay afloat in the sea! With each gasp for breath, his throat stung with salty water.

Then a giant wall of water pounded him down, down, down. And all was black.

CHAPTER XXXII: Unlucky to Be Alive

hen Digory next opened his eyes, he had no idea where he was or how he'd gotten there. He found himself warm and snug in a strange bed, under an old tattered quilt that smelled of salt, smoke, and fish oil. His head ached and his throat burned, and there was shooting pain in his knee. He struggled to get up out of the bed but nearly fell over.

An old woman laid a wrinkled hand on his shoulder.

"Rest, boy," she told him, bringing a mug of snail tea to his lips. "You nearly drowned."

Digory tried to remember what had happened, but his mind drew a blank.

"Where am I?" he said shakily, looking around the dimly lit room.

"You're in Plymouth Town, duck," the old woman replied. "In Kip Finn the fish seller's cottage. And there he be, old Kip himself, standing by the fire. Lucky to be alive, you are, lad."

"We're all of us lucky to be alive after that evil storm," Kip Finn agreed as he came and stood beside the bed. "Lost most of the tiles from our roof, we did! Never in all me seventy years 'ave I seen the sea and the sky in such a fury. They say there are hundreds of boats gone missing and bodies piled high along the quay. 'Twas a miracle they were able to pull you from the waves on such an evil night, that it was, lad."

"But . . . but what of the boatman and the others?" Digory asked, his voice groggy and his head reeling.

The old fish seller shrugged. "Can't say. Them that brought ye up onto the beach left ye there for us to find."

"And Master Henry?" Digory cried weakly. "What of Master Henry?"

"Let the boy rest now," the old woman said, shooing her husband away. She turned back to Digory. "Close yer eyes and rest now, lamb. Ye need to sleep."

Digory did as he was told, for he was still so very tired. He fell back into a sound and dreamless sleep. When he awoke, hours later, or perhaps it was days, he found the old woman snoring beside the fire with her knitting in her lap. The old man was nowhere to be seen. As Digory sat up in the bed, he tried to remember what had happened.

Where was Cubby? Where was Master Henry? And what happened to the boatman and the keepers?

I must get back to the inn and find Cubby, he thought. He glanced down and saw that he was wearing a large muslin shirt that was not his own. He looked around the room that was a clutter of mismatched teacups, chipped china plates, baskets of seashells, and buckets filled with fish bones.

When Digory spotted his clothes draped over a large spinning wheel before the fire, he slipped out from under the quilt and crept out of the bed. The floorboards creaked loudly as he limped across the room. Looking down, he noticed that his legs and arms were badly bruised and there was a deep gash above his left knee.

The old woman stirred and mumbled in her sleep. Digory silently reached for his clothes. He struggled into his breeches and headed out the door.

Once outside, Digory stopped short and stared at the destruction all around him. Could this really be the same Plymouth? The sun was shining under a blue, cloudless sky, but the street had disappeared and was replaced by piles of rubble and wreckage: lumber, bricks, and broken furniture, as far as the eye could see. Rooftops had been torn off completely. Windows were smashed and shutters ripped off their hinges. There was not one chimney left on a house. Those who had survived were silently sifting through the rubble that had once been their lives.

As Digory slowly found his way down the street, a sickening feeling took hold of him. Never before had he seen such devastation. He had to find Cubby right away.

"Can you tell me the way to the White Owl Inn?" Digory asked a man who was pushing a cart full of bricks. But the man shook his head and kept on walking.

"Please, miss," Digory begged of a young woman who was picking through a pile of rubble. "Have you heard any news of the White Owl Inn?"

"I've heard nothing but my mother's wails," answered the woman. "For this place where you stand was my father's tavern." She pulled a chipped mug from the heap and started to cry.

Digory fought back his own tears. How was he to find the inn? He began wandering from one pile of rubble to the next, when his eyes fixed on a familiar scene in the distance. It was the bluff, Plymouth Hoe, where he and Cubby and Master Henry had first seen the lighthouse on their return to Plymouth.

His heart raced as a man looked out over the water through a spyglass, and Digory scrambled over a pile of timber and bricks to join him.

"Please, sir," Digory pleaded. "Might I borrow your glass to look at the Light?"

"You can look all you like, lad," the man said, handing him the glass. "But you'll not see the Eddystone Light, not ever again."

"What do you mean, sir?" Digory cried as he brought the glass to his eye.

"She's not there," the man said, shaken. "She's just not there!"

"That's impossible!" Digory gasped. "She must be there! She must!" But the more he searched through the glass, the more he understood that the man spoke the truth. For all he could see was the smooth span of the ocean spreading out across the horizon, save for the reddish reef that jutted up from the waves. It was as if the little lighthouse had never been there! As if it had all been a dream.

"They say that the Jester himself was out there last night," Digory heard the man say. "Imagine being in that tower when it came down."

Digory could listen no more. He returned the glass to the man and ran away. He ran past broken crockery, fallen timbers, and shards of glass. He kept on running. When he finally got to the Barbican steps, he sank down and buried his face in his hands. Then he sobbed as if his heart would break. Master Henry was gone! How could that be?

"All or nothing, that's what you said!" Digory cried as he lifted his face up to the blue sky above. "But where did it get you? You gave your all and now there is nothing!"

Digory looked out over the beach at the many splintered ships that were piled high upon it. Each one was smashed and broken beyond repair, as if a giant had walked across the water, crushing everything in his path and tossing it up onto the sand.

A gull lay dead at the bottom of the steps, a gaping wound in its neck. Digory sucked in another sob. He felt as broken as the smashed ships, as wounded as the gull that would never fly again. Master Henry, whom he had come to love and admire, was gone. How could someone so full of life be dead?

With another pang of sadness he thought of his father. He remembered how strong and full of vigor he had always been. But the sea had taken him as well, just as it had taken his mother, his uncle, and his grandfather, too.

"The sea has taken everyone I love," he said aloud. And suddenly he thought of Cubby. He had to find Cubby right away! He got to his feet and ran toward the street. He darted around the wreckage looking for the White Owl Inn, but when he reached the street, there was nothing he could recognize.

"Please, mistress, can you point out the White Owl Inn?" he asked a woman who was carrying a large bundle of rags on her back.

"The White Owl?" she whispered, laying a shaky hand on Digory's arm. "Why, 'tis over there. They've been pulling bodies from it all day." She pointed across the street to a building that had collapsed upon itself and was now just another mountain of rubble.

On top of the broken heap was a sign with a large white owl painted on it. The owl's eyes were open, as if it were staring up at the sky.

"It can't be!" Digory cried, breaking away from the woman and running across the street. "Cubby! Cubby!" he shouted. He dug into the rubble with his bare hands. "Where are you, Cubby?" he pleaded.

"Come away with you now, lad," a man covered in dust called as he pulled Digory back. "Can you not see how dangerous it is to be poking around here?"

"But my brother," Digory tried to explain. "He was staying at the inn. I thought he'd be safe here. I have to find him! I have to help him!"

"There's nothing you can do now, lad," the man said gently. "No one's coming out of there alive today. We pulled out twenty dead from here already."

"Did you pull out my brother?" Digory asked, taking all his strength to find the words. "He's a small boy with red hair and freckles. And he has a dog with a blue parrot riding on its back."

The man shook his head no and pointed down the street to the one stone building that was still standing. "They are bringing all the bodies to the blacksmith's shop. If he was one of them pulled out today, he'd be there."

Digory stumbled toward the stone building, heart heavy with dread.

He recalled the old fish seller saying how lucky they'd all been to survive the storm. But what was lucky about it if everyone Digory ever loved was gone? Unlucky to be alive — that was more like it, Digory thought as he smelled the fresh horse manure beside the blacksmith's shop. From inside came the harrowing sound of a woman's wails. Digory shuddered and shrank back away from the building.

How was he to go in there? How was he to face seeing what the storm had done to his little brother? He crouched beside a wall, unable to move. An hour went by and then another. The sky was still a brilliant blue with not a cloud on the horizon. Digory bowed his head, unable to look at such a bright, beautiful day, when he heard a voice that made his heart leap.

"Yo, ho, ho! Nincompoop off the mizzen!"

CHAPTER XXXIII: The Shanty

Digory rose with a start. "Mizzen!" he called out. Then he noticed a sailor with a black eye and a bloodstained bandage wrapped around his head. A bright blue parrot was perched on his shoulder squawking, "Yo, ho, ho!"

"What are you doing with Mizzen?" Digory cried. "And what have you done with my brother, Cubby? He was staying at the White Owl."

The sailor's face fell. "Lost half our crew there last night," he said hoarsely. "Every sailor expects to be taken in a storm, but not on land. My God, not on land . . ." His voice trailed off.

"And my brother?" Digory pleaded. "Where is my brother?"

"The little carrottop in a big blue coat?"

Digory nodded as he wiped at his eyes.

"He's got me minding his parrot while his arm is being tended to," the sailor said. "There's a doctor set up shop, setting bones and such, in a coffeehouse around the corner."

"Then he's alive?" Digory cried, clutching the man's sleeve.

"Oh, he's alive, all right. Said he'd run out into the street to look for his dog, just before the building come down," the sailor explained. "He got banged up good from the timbers falling around him, but he made it out all right. That dog of his saved his life. When we found him and his dog, he was holding on to his birdcage and a leather case for dear life."

Digory followed the sailor around the corner to one of the few buildings left on the street. Once inside, he found it crowded with bloodied and bruised people. It seemed as if all of Plymouth was crammed inside its walls. Many were moaning and crying out in pain or for lost loved ones. Others stood shaken and silent. And still others lay unconscious on makeshift cots. But Digory's heart leaped when he heard a familiar voice calling him from across the room.

"Digory! Digory!" Cubby cried.

Though his freckled face was covered in cuts and bruises and his arm was in a sling, Cubby's grin was as wide as ever on seeing his brother alive.

"Are you all right?" Digory cried, reaching out for him and petting Fishbone, who wildly licked Digory's face. The dog's tail wagged so hard, he knocked a cup off a table.

The sailor returned Mizzen to his cage on the floor beside Cubby and then disappeared into the crowd. Meanwhile, the two brothers lost no time in telling each other their stories of all that had happened during their time apart.

A sudden commotion arose at the door as two sailors burst into the room. "We've just heard the news," one of them cried. "They say the Eddystone Light is no more!"

Digory shuddered at the sound of the collective gasp that followed.

"How shall we manage that monster reef now?" someone cried.

"Without the Light we've no chance of staying clear of those rocks!"

"The Widow Maker is back!"

"They say that the Jester himself was swept out to sea with his tower!" the sailor continued.

Digory swallowed back a sob as he looked at Cubby's stricken face.

"God save his soul!" a sailor shouted. "His beacon guided our ship in last night!"

"His beacon guided us all," another added.

"Three cheers for Henry Winstanley!"

"Hear! Hear!" The room erupted. "Three cheers for the Jester and his Eddystone Light!"

Digory put his arm around his little brother.

"You'll have to move on now, lads," a man carrying a bundle of rags told them. "There are many more injured who need to come in."

Digory stared back numbly. Just where were they to "move on" to? No one in Plymouth would hire them now, not with such devastation everywhere. And without Master Henry they had nothing and no one to return to.

Digory picked up Mizzen's cage, and he and Cubby began to inch their way through the crowded room. A baby shrieked in its mother's arms. "Hush, now, hush," the woman said, trying to quiet her child.

Digory had almost reached the door when he heard someone say, "I've just the shanty to calm the babe."

The voice sounded so familiar, Digory froze in place. His heart pounded wildly as the man began to sing the old shanty:

"*Dance to your daddy,*
My little laddie.
Dance to your daddy,
My little man."

CHAPTER XXXIV: A Radiant Future

he baby quieted as the man continued to sing:

> *"Thou shall have a fish,*
> *Thou shall have a fin,*
> *Thou shall have a haddock,*
> *When the boat comes in."*

"Do you hear that?" gasped Cubby.

Digory searched the room full of faces until he spotted the man who was singing. He was lying on a cot with his leg wrapped in bloody rags. His hair was matted and dirty, and his face unshaven. But his smile was unmistakable. It was the same sad smile that Digory had always loved. And his eyes were as green as Digory's own.

"Father!" Digory shouted as he and Cubby pushed through the crowd to reach him. "Father! Oh, Father!" he and Cubby cried together.

Nicholas Beale's handsome, weathered face broke into a radiant smile at the sight of his sons before him. His big, strong arms wrapped around them. He couldn't hold them tight enough. And he couldn't stop looking at them.

"Am I dreaming?" he said. "Whatever are you two doing here?"

"We had news of the *Flying Cloud* wrecking in Yarmouth," Digory began. "Aunt Alice could no longer keep us, so she sent us to look for you."

"There was no way to get word home. I departed on the *Flying Cloud*, but I never boarded her for the return voyage," their father explained. "I fell sick with fever in Genoa and had to stay behind. I only got to Plymouth yesterday in the midst of that horrific storm. How long have you been here?"

It was then that Digory told his father how Aunt Alice sent him to Plymouth, and about their harrowing journey there, and Master Death and the press-gang, and how Master Henry saved them from prison and took them to the Magic House to live and work. He told him how Master Henry had discovered Digory's talent for drawing and had taken him on as his apprentice. Digory told his father about the lighthouse and the dangerous trip out to Eddystone.

"Master Henry wouldn't leave the reef," Digory said, fighting back his tears. "The keeper tried to warn him, but he wouldn't listen. We lit the candles together. But when he saw a boat in the distance, he decided to stay to keep the tower lit. But the storm was too strong. Now he and his lighthouse are gone!"

Color rushed to his father's face, for suddenly he understood. "You were out on the Eddystone in that storm? Then it was you and your Master Henry who saved my life and the lives of our crew," his father told him. "For that was our ship that came around the Stone late yesterday. It was only because of the light from the tower that we were able to steer clear of the Eddystone Reef and make it back into the harbor. There were over one hundred of us on that ship. Many of them are in here now." He gazed at the sailors who stood close by.

"So what was he like, son, this Jester of Littlebury?" Digory heard his father ask.

The tears came to Digory's eyes as he struggled to answer. He pictured Master Henry back in his workshop, creating his amazing gadgets and rides for the Magic House, his voice crackling with excitement as he talked of his many projects and plans.

He thought of the love and caring the master had shown when he and Cubby had no one to turn to. And he thought of the hope Master Henry's words had given him, words he would never forget. "Your future is as radiant as you see it. . . ."

But most vivid to Digory was his memory of the master standing so bold and brave in his lantern room, in all that glorious light. Again Digory glanced around at the many sailors who owed their lives to the Jester of Littlebury. But when he looked at his father, he realized the most important thing of all. Thanks to Master Henry, his father was alive! Digory finally understood. It was not all for nothing. It had never been that.

"He was unlike anyone I've ever met," Digory finally answered.

His father nodded. "And to light that rock and stay out there in that storm. Why, he must have been . . ."

"Fearless," Digory finished the sentence for him. "He was fearless."

Everyone was quiet for a moment.

"And what's this you're carrying?" Their father broke through the silence, tapping on the leather tube across Cubby's chest.

In all of the commotion Digory had forgotten about the case! He quickly slid it off Cubby's shoulder and opened the lid. He took out two rolled papers. With a pang of sadness he recognized the master's stylish script.

"These must be the documents Master Henry spoke of," Digory murmured. "They are signed by him," he said, reading the signature.

"How could you know that?" his father asked.

"Because I can read," Digory said proudly. "Mistress Elizabeth taught Cubby and me our letters."

Nicholas Beale smiled in awe at his eldest son. "I never thought I'd see the day a child of mine could read! Go on, Digory, read the words aloud."

Digory looked back down at the paper and cleared his throat.

"'To Mistress Henry Winstanley of Littlebury,'" he began.

People around them grew quiet at the mention of the master's name. Digory continued to read.

My dearest Elizabeth,

If you receive news that I am gone, please know that it was never my intention to leave you. Someone must stay in the tower to keep the light, and I pray to God it will hold. But should it not, I want you to remember what I've always told you — that you have been my light, my beacon through so many storms. If I am to perish tonight it is with a full heart, full of love, my dear, for you.

Your most grateful and adoring husband,

Henry

A sad silence hung over the room. No one spoke. No one moved. Then Digory lowered the first paper and picked up the second. He swallowed hard and began to read:

To Digory Beale,

Though I have been your master and you my apprentice, it is you who have taught me so very much. You've opened my eyes and my heart to what it's like to be a father to a brave boy with a keen mind and a noble heart.

I am leaving you some coin and my compass to give you some direction, even though I trust you are a clever lad and will find your way in the world on your own. Whatever happens, wherever I may be when you read this, do not be sad, for I have lived the life I chose. I had the chance to light the reef and I took it.

Farewell, my young friend, and remember: c'est tout ou rien.

Henry Winstanley

Digory turned the case over and gave it a shake. A shower of silver coins poured out along with the small brass compass.

"I never saw so much silver in all me life!" Cubby cried, picking up the coins that had fallen to the floor.

"The master told me to keep the coins," Digory said quietly. "But I thought there'd be just enough to buy us two seats on a coach back to Littlebury."

"Why, there's enough silver here to buy an entire coach and four!" his father exclaimed.

Tears filled Digory's eyes as he read the letters on the face of the compass, and he remembered back to the day Master Henry had taught to him how to read it.

"If we follow the W it will direct us west," Digory said, swallowing hard. "Back to Mousehole."

"Can we go home now, Father?" Cubby pleaded.

"Aye, as soon as I am well," their father said. "And after we deliver Master Henry's letter back to his wife in Littlebury," he added.

"When we get back to Mousehole, will we have to live with Aunt Alice in her smoky cottage again?" asked Cubby.

"Nay." His father smiled. "We've enough silver here to rent us a fine cottage down by the harbor."

"With a chimney that don't smoke?" Cubby asked hopefully.

"Aye." His father laughed. "With a chimney that don't smoke."

"And a window," Digory said, smiling through his tears. "It must have a window to let in the light."

"Yes," said his father. "With a window to let in the light."

Six weeks later, five weary travelers disembarked from a boat in Mounts Bay. They made an unusual sight as they walked up the cobbled streets of the sleepy little village of Mousehole. There was a handsome man with a slight limp, a tall, thin boy with black hair and ocean-green eyes, and a smaller boy in a big wool coat with a carrot-colored ponytail. Following close behind them was a shaggy dog with a crooked smile and a bright blue parrot perched on his head.

As they rounded a familiar street, the taller boy looked up at the smoke that curled from a chimney top. He stared hard with all of his attention. Where the others saw only smoke, he saw a picture take shape. It was a tower, wide at the bottom, thinning at the top. A lighthouse. The smoky tower wiggled and waved in the air. Then the boy blinked, and the vision disappeared on the breeze before him.

Later that day in the sand on the beach over-looking the bay, he would draw it back to life for his many cousins to see. And every day after that, for the rest of his life, he would carry a small brass compass in his pocket along with a picture of the light in his heart, a light as bright as the sixty candles that once burned atop a brave little lighthouse on the Eddystone Reef.

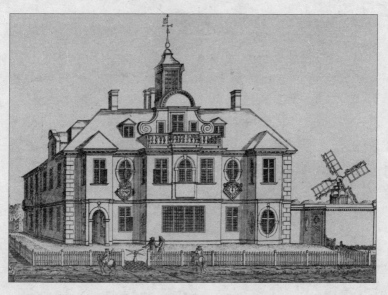

Henry Winstanley's House of Wonders in Littlebury, Essex, in England.

AUTHOR'S NOTE

THE MAGIC HOUSE IN LITTLEBURY

This story was inspired by the life and times of a very real person — Henry Winstanley, artist, architect, gadgeteer, and showman. Henry was born in 1644 in Saffron Walden, England. In 1683, he married Elizabeth Taylor, and they built a house in the village of Littlebury. It was in this house that Henry created many of his one-of-a-kind gadgets and amusements, including a self-opening door, a clockwork ghost, trick mirrors, musical fountains, the world's first robotic butler, and the forerunner to the roller coaster.

The Winstanley house was topped with a magnificent lantern and further decorated with whirligigs and weather vanes. A musical windmill turned in the garden. The effect was so whimsical that people passing by on the Coach Road stopped to stare. A turnstile was soon added and admission of one shilling per person was charged to walk through Winstanley's House of Wonders, or the Magic House or Smiling House, as it was sometimes called. Thus was born one of the first fun houses in England and the forerunner of our amusement parks of today.

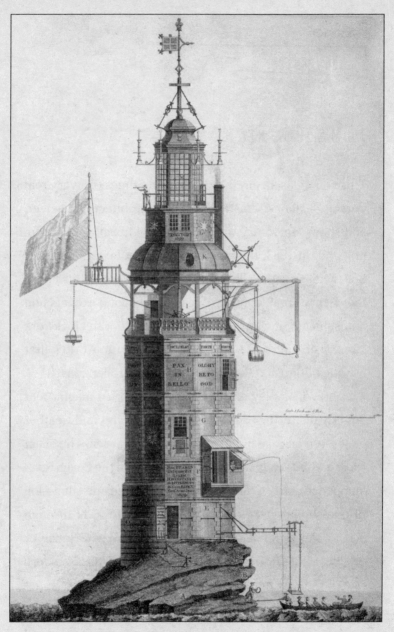

The Eddystone Light, as it stood on the Eddystone Reef in 1699.

Winstanley's House of Wonders was a huge success, and even King Charles took notice. He commissioned Henry to build a fun fair entertainment for him in Piccadilly. It was known as Winstanley's Waterworks and consisted of trick fountains and firework displays that dazzled all of London. As people flocked to see it, Henry became one of England's most famous showmen. He was nick-named the Jester of Littlebury.

A Light on "The Widow Maker"

Besides his gadgeteering, Henry Winstanley's passion for art and architecture led him to his most challenging project yet — to put a lighthouse on the Eddystone Reef. It was a project that many called madness, for the Eddystone was fourteen miles from Plymouth's shores and one of the deadliest reefs on the English coast. They called it "The Widow Maker."

It was the age of sail. In 1695, with no modern navigational instruments, as many as fifty ships a year were wrecked on the Eddystone Reef. Hundreds of sailors lost their lives, and legends of the deadly reef spread all along the coast. Henry Winstanley, never one to be put off by a challenge, decided that he was the man to tame the killer reef.

In the early summer of 1696, the Jester headed to Plymouth armed with his designs. The lighthouse he envisioned was no ordinary, practical-looking structure but a graceful, whimsical tower, looking more like something out of a fairy tale. It was a lighthouse that only Henry Winstanley could have dreamed up.

The project was to consume him for the next three years. The boat ride out to the reef was a grueling six to seven hours, with the men often having to resort to oars in the strong currents. Once they did reach the reef, there was no guarantee they could land, and often they had to seek shelter along the coast.

The work itself seemed all but impossible. How were they to pierce the ironlike rock when the only available tools were picks and axes? It took the strongest, heartiest men of Cornwall and Devon to accomplish such a punishing task. Through all the difficulties, Winstanley's determination never flagged. With his stories, conjuring tricks, and high spirits, he cheered his men on through the entire project.

Finally, on November 14, 1698, Henry Winstanley was able to do what no person had ever done before him. He climbed up to his lantern room and lit the first candle that was to shine on the Eddystone Reef. The world's first rock (or caisson) lighthouse was lit.

As fishermen spread the word, people rushed to the beaches. Crowds swarmed Plymouth Hoe to catch a glimpse of the brightness through their telescopes. Henry

Winstanley was toasted as a hero and given a silver replica of the lighthouse in miniature, made as a standing salt (meant to hold salt and sugar).

The Storm of the Century

Over the next five years, not one ship was lost on the Eddystone Reef, due to the light from Henry Winstanley's beacon. Winstanley himself often traveled back and forth from Littlebury to Plymouth to make repairs on his lighthouse. When word reached him that the keepers he had hired were worried about the tower's ability to withstand another storm, Henry once again traveled out to Plymouth for what was to be his final journey.

Little could he have known when he bragged about the strength of his lighthouse and uttered the words "I should only wish to be there in the greatest storm that ever blew under the face of the heavens" that his wish was about to be granted. He had no way of knowing that the worst storm ever to ravage England's coast, the "Storm of the Century" as the writer Daniel Defoe would later describe it, was barreling straight for the Eddystone Reef.

On November 26, 1703, the night the storm hit, the wind tore all across England with a violence that seemed supernatural. The fury coming off the Atlantic was a combination of hurricane, tornado, and cyclone. Eight hundred houses were destroyed and thousands more damaged. Hundreds of thousands of trees were uprooted. Fifteen thousand sheep were killed as miles of countryside were flooded.

In the West Country alone, over one hundred and fifty ships were lost that night and eight thousand sailors were said to have drowned.

Back in Littlebury, when a strong gust came through a window at the Magic House, it knocked the silver replica of the lighthouse onto the floor. Elizabeth Winstanley said that when she saw the little lighthouse in pieces she knew it was a sign that her Henry was dead.

Indeed, the Eddystone lighthouse, along with all those within her, was swept out to sea sometime between midnight and seven in the morning on November 27, 1703. Henry Winstanley; James Bound, the boatman; the workmen; and the keepers were never seen again.

Two nights later, the *Winchelsea*, bound from Virginia with a cargo of tobacco, wrecked on the Eddystone Reef. Only two of the crew survived. It was the first ship in five years' time to wreck on the Eddystone's deadly rocks. "The Widow Maker" was back.

Henry's Gift to the World

Henry Winstanley believed that his lighthouse could withstand any storm. He paid the ultimate price for his miscalculations. But it was his creativity, energy, and determination that inspired others to go on to rebuild the Eddystone Light as well as other rock lighthouses all over the world.

Henry Winstanley saved hundreds of lives in his life-time and thousands more since. The Eddystone Light recently celebrated its three-hundredth birthday. The Jester of Littlebury is all but forgotten, though the light from his magical mind and unique spirit still shines on our world today.

Henry Winstanley, a self-portrait.

This map of England in 1700 highlights places where the story is set.
It also shows England in relation to the world (bottom right).

GLOSSARY

BARNACLE: any of various crustaceans that permanently affix themselves to boat hulls and rocks.

BILGEWATER: water that collects in the bilge of a ship; thus, putrid water.

BLUFF: a high, steep bank.

BOATSWAIN: a petty officer on a merchant ship who controls the work of the other seamen.

BREECHES: trousers that end at or just below the knee.

CHAMBER POT: a small bowl or pot kept under the bed and used as a toilet at night.

CHANDLER: one who makes or sells candles and soap.

CHANNEL: a narrow part of the sea running between two close masses of land.

CONSTABLE: a policeman.

COPPERS: slang for copper coins, particularly the large cents and half cents.

CORNISHMAN: a native of Cornwall.

CORPSE: a dead body.

COXSWAIN: the sailor who steers and takes charge of both crew and boat.

FAIR MAIDENS: Cornish expression for dried, salted pilchard fish.

GADGETEER: a person who designs and builds gadgets.

GALE: a strong wind from 32 to 63 miles per hour.

GIBBET: an upright post with an extending arm used for hanging criminals; a gallows.

GNEISS (pronounced like *nice*): a reddish-colored rock; the rock on which Henry Winstanley built his lighthouse.

HIGHWAYMAN: a highjacker or thief who robs travelers on a road.

HOGSHEAD: a large barrel holding up to 63 gallons.

INFRACTION: a violation of a law; a minor offense.

JESTER: a servant dressed as a clown employed to entertain a king or nobleman in the Middle Ages.

MICHAELMAS: a Christian feast observed on September 29 in honor of the archangel Michael.

MILLER: one who owns, operates, or works in a mill that grinds grain into flour.

PINCH: slang for steal.

PENCE: a penny.

PILCHARD: an oily sea fish.

PRESS-GANG: a group of sailors who recruited for their ship using violence and intimidation. This was a particular threat for civilian men in port towns in times of war.

REEF: an underwater chain of rocks or coral that juts out slightly from the surface of the water and creates a hazardous obstruction.

RICKETY: broken down, weak, and shaky.

SCULLERY MAID: the lowest ranking of female servants. The scullery maid assists the kitchen maid and performs the most physical and disagreeable tasks — such as cleaning the floors, stoves, and sinks, and scrubbing pots and dishes.

SHILLING: a former unit of money in the United Kingdom.

SNAIL TEA: Chinese tea made from a bud that is shapped like a snail.

SQUIRE: an English country gentleman; often the chief landowner in the district.

TALLOWS: candles made of tallow, a waxy fat.

TANKARD: a large drinking mug.

TINCTURE: a medicinal substance in an alcohol base.

TOPIARY: plants or bushes trained, cut, or trimmed into ornamental shapes.

TWILL: a type of weave.

WAGE: a salary; payment in exchange for labor.

WAISTCOAT: a vest.

WHIST: a card game.

WINDOW TAX: a tax levied on windows in England in 1696 by William III to raise money. Many houses bricked their windows to avoid the tax.

SHIP'S GLOSSARY

Bow: the forward part of a boat.

Crow's nest: a platform for a lookout at or near the top of the mast.

Figurehead: an ornamental figure on the bow of the boat.

Ketch: a sailboat with two masts.

Hull: the body of a ship that provides the buoyancy to keep it afloat.

Jib: a triangular headsail mounted to the head stay.

Jolly boat: a medium-size boat onboard a ship used for general work.

Mast: a vertical pole holding up the sails.

Mizzenmast: third mast from the bow in a vessel having three or more masts.

Port: the left side of a ship looking forward.

Ratlines: any of the small ropes fastened horizontally to the shrouds of a ship and forming a ladder for going aloft.

Shroud: one of the ropes leading from a ship's mastheads to give lateral support to the masts. Shrouds are usually found in pairs.

Starboard: the right side of a ship looking forward.

Stern: the rear or aft part of the ship.

BIBLIOGRAPHY

BARNES, ALISON. *Henry Winstanley: Artist, Inventor and Light-house-builder.* Plymouth: Tourist Information Service and Saffron Walden Museum, Uttlesford District Council and Plymouth City Museum, 2003.

BEER, TREVOR AND ENDYMION. *Birds of Cornwall.* Cornwall: Tor Mark Press, 1999.

BEER, TREVOR AND ENDYMION. *Wild Flowers of the Cornish Coast.* Cornwall: Tor Mark Press, 1999.

BLAKE, GEORGE. *British Ships and Shipbuilders.* London: Collins, 1946.

HOGG, GARRY. *Facets of the English Scene.* Devon: David & Charles, 1973.

HUNT, ROBERT. *Cornish Folklore.* Cornwall: Tor Mark Press, 2000.

MAJDALANY, FRED. *The Eddystone Light.* Boston: Houghton Mifflin, 1960.

MUIR, RICHARD. *The English Village.* New York: Thames and Hudson, 1980.

PALMER, MIKE. *Eddystone 300: The Finger of Light.* Cornwall: Palmridge Publishing, 1998.

PORTERPUB, ROY. *English Society in the Eighteenth Century.* London: Penguin Books, 1982.

SEMMENS, JASSON. *Eddystone: 300 Years*. Cornwall: Fowey Rare
    Books/Alexander and Associates, 1998.
TRURAN, CHRISTINE. *A Short Cornish Dictionary*. Cornwall: Truran,
    1986.

⊷⊷⊷

ART CREDITS